# THE COIN

# THE COIN

**SANDEEP SHARMA**

rg books

Anybook

The Coin (Novel)


Price in india : ₹ 99
Price out side india : $ 5

Published By :

***Redgrab books***
942, Mutthiganj, Allahabad, 211003
Website : www.redgrabbooks.com
E-mail : contact@redgrabbooks.com

&

***Anybook***
G 248, 2nd floor, Sector 63
Noida - 201301, U.P.
Website : www.anybook.org
E-mail : contactanybook@gmail.com

ISBN : 978-93-87390-26-3
Printed at : ThomsonPress (India) Limited, New Delhi
Cover design : PixelR8 Studios
Cover Photo : Shutterstock
Edition : First, Paperback, March 2018 (5100 copies)

*I dedicate this book to all those dreamers*
*who chose to stand against the world*
*to achieve their dreams.*

# CONTENT

# PROLOGUE

You wait for it to rest. You wait patiently, adjusts the direction of light falling over it. A very strange tickling of excitement is inducing a beautiful smile over your face. Slowly, it is resting; the water in which you want to see your reflection is slowly resting. At any moment, this waving reflection of yours will attain a calm position.

"Don't lean too much, Sandy." A shout of his father made him conscious about his madness but till that moment, the madness has taken control over the sanity. He leaned a little more, totally ignoring the world around.

Sandy, 12 years old boy was having perfect Sunday morning till his father, Avnish Batra's phone buzzed. They were out for fishing. Avnish was a businessman and in the name of a family he had only his son and a maid, whom he treated as his sister. Every second Sunday, Avnish used to postpone every meeting of his just to spend some quality time with his son. Although he had given strict instructions to everyone, not to call him while he was out but this time, something was surely serious.

Sandy loved water. There was some unexplained relation of his with the water. Whenever he is around a lake, he becomes the happiest person on earth. He loved to see his reflection over the surface of it. It was, as if, he is watching something really special, something that can't be seen or felt by anyone else, except him. After the sudden death of Avnish's wife, Avnish became little conscious about his son so he always kept an eye on his son. But today, Avnish was busy in something that took his attention away.

Sandy was waiting patiently, as he knew, within few seconds, the water will become silent. He was leaning through the deck and below him was just water of almost 20 feet in depth. He leaned a little more as he doesn't want to miss the magical feeling. He was almost touching the surface of the water with his nose.

Reflection started to clear out but something was eerie about it. Sandy was not feeling the same as he always does. The moment turbulence calmed, his reflection begins to clear out but somehow, it wasn't him. Suddenly the turbulence increased, the reflection started to come closer. Then he realized, it wasn't him, it wasn't the reflection anymore. Turbulence kept on increasing as the pair of closed eyes came closer to Sandy, from below the water surface and hits on his face. Loud scream of his son made Avnish throw his mobile phone aside and run to fetch the drowning child.

# 1

*He couldn't breathe. He tried hard, but the air wasn't sufficient to make him feel relaxed and provide the required oxygen for his body to function. He gasped. Beads of sweat trickled down his face. He tried to pull himself off his bed. He attempted to at least throw the blanket off his legs, but nothing worked. At that moment, something that was popularly known as sleep paralysis attacked him. He knew that if no one came into the room, he would start to hallucinate. His bad past would hover in front of him, haunting him. All those faces, all those killings, everything that he was shameful of would start to replay in front of his eyes like a movie on a loop. Only he knew how hard and far he had ran to forget and forgive himself for all those dead people.*

*His body felt as if it was losing his soul. It felt like witnessing a quiet and calm death, like something was about to rise out of his body. Just then, he heard a familiar voice – that of his father's.*

*"Shhh... relax, you are all right, my son." His father shook him hard to wake him up from his 'horrifying' sleep.*

*At the age of fourteen, he had seen a lot in his life, a lot more than one could expect for a teenager. He sweated as if he was in an extremely humid place. He clutched his father's waist and tried to forget what he had seen. It was not his first time he had seen such visions, but they were as horrifying.*

*He had so many questions he wanted to ask, but he ventured none. He clenched his teeth and tried to stop the tears falling down his eyes. 'He is stronger than he thinks he is,' he reminded himself.*

He jumped off the bed in a sudden movement and went into the kitchen. He had always wanted a two bedroom apartment with a basement. He had searched long and far for the perfect 'lonely' location and when he found his dream house, he negotiated with the broker.

The fierce fight between him and his thoughts required all of his strength to sustain, so much that even those few steps towards the kitchen felt difficult. He picked up a glass, poured water into it, and drank in a single gulp. The duel in his mind made him want to cool down. He poured another glass and emptied it on his head.

He fell on the floor. He wanted to cry, but couldn't. *Emotion makes you weak, and trust me, you aren't!'* His father's words echoed every time in his ears when he wanted to cry. The water seemed to freshen up his mind and drive away the rampaging conflict. *'Let's get back to the work!'* He placed the glass back in its place and moved to his workplace -- the basement.

There was always something strange in his walk whenever he came down to his basement. He felt powerful as if he could do anything. But he wasn't here to do something that needed his power; he just wanted to have answers because questions weren't the only thing he couldn't sustain. *Your answers lie in your acts,* his father used to say.

He could now hear the loud breathing come from the darkest corner of the basement, just below the stairs. Except for the occasional squeaking of the rats, the basement reeked of silence.

"Who are you?"

Fear gave birth to anxiety and that would be the thing that could destroy one's mental abilities. While he descended down the stairs, he knew that his prey was tied on the wooden chair by firm, strong ropes and was afraid of him. The thought alone made him feel relaxed.

"Who are you? Why have you bought me here?" His prey asked again. This time it sounded as if his anxiety was at its peak.

He did not reply. Neither did he make any eye contact. He kept his head low and searched for something throughout the basement. He got a chair to sit and faced his prey, who sat only a few feet away from him.

"Why?" His prey asked again. His voice came as if in a whisper. "Why? Well, I don't know." He raised his hands up and gave the prey a chance to look at his hunter. His prey seemed shocked to see his face because he looked ordinary. Pretty ordinary. Nobody could have accepted a decent kind of boy one could find on their neighbourhood to be a hunter. The only thing about his prey that frightened him was his deep, clear, firm voice, though now rendered nearly inaudible. His prey went silent. Perhaps he was confused.

"Would you like to hear a story?" he asked.

"NO. Just leave me alone. I want to go back to my home." Somewhere, he knew that the fear had left his prey and replaced by anger. He read the warning in those words and left his chair to find another thing – an axe. "Okay… Listen… Okay, I will listen to your story…. I am sorry…… don't do this…" His prey started crying once he saw the axe. He kept the axe in his sight and sat again on the chair.

"So here it goes…"

*Let me tell you the incident from where a child's life changed. It was 1988, 31st August. Flora and fauna were abundant at that place – a beautiful treat for the eyes of a normal man living a normal life in an urban surrounding. Cool breeze and the sound of sparkling water were the highlights of that place; for him though, things were a bit different. Hot air to feel, smoke to breathe, sweat to smell, burning glass to watch, and*

*thirsty throat – that was his daily routine.He was nine-years-old and the last image of his parents in his thoughts was of a wailing mother and a drunken father putting his thumb print on some papers. He was actually sold for two-hundred-and-fifty rupees to an owner of a manufacturing firm that used children to make bangles for them in the remote areas of India.*

*He saw the cruel side of humanity pretty early in his life. Twelve hours of working in front of the furnace, a two-time food that barely fulfilled the hunger, and abusing men all over the place. There was no such concept of a friend there. He knew only one thing: Work hard if you want to survive.*

*There was only one face that was familiar to hin. Rajesh. He was sixteen-years-old and perhaps the only one there who knew how to read and write. Every night, he used to write something in his diary. Rajesh loved it and sometimes, when lonely at night, he used to talk to it as well. That was the time when this child had heard his name. Rajesh had never told him.*

*They never talked to each other as their masters didn't allow anyone to talk, but they did share a bonding, which could be said as Rajesh's worst mistake.*

*That day was as normal as their routine. All of them drank their own sweat and creating the world's most famous bangles. But today, the child wasn't feeling so well. The masters saw that the efficiency of the child wasn't up to the mark. That made one of them come forward and slap the child hard. Rajesh sat opposite the child, watching everything, but silent as everyone else.*

*The master didn't look back when the child fell on the ground and fainted. Rajesh saw him and reacted in*

*an instance – perhaps because of fondness or a reaction to stimuli – but that instant movement pushed the master, making him lose his balance. Rajesh stood dumbstruck for a moment. He saw his master fall towards the furnace, but before he could fall over it, he fell chest-first into an iron rod, which penetrated him. The master died in that moment.*

"So how was it?" he asked in excitement to his prey.

The prey said nothing and remained silent.

"I know……… I know what you are thinking." He had kept rotating the axe on the ground while talking. "You think that story is bullshit because it was incomplete." He stopped rotating the axe and made his grip firm on the handle. "Actually, the story isn't incomplete, but you know what……" He left his chair. That made his prey feel a strange kind of fear.. "The problem is the sudden death. No one likes to hear about sudden deaths or may be, no one likes it." He picked up his axe and stabbed with the sharp side of it on the right leg of his prey, which made the latter cry hard.All he could do now was to wait and see the enormous amount of blood flow out of his limb.

# 2

He could still hear the gateman's footsteps as the latter paced to and fro. He observed his movements – seven steps up and seven down. According to his generalized calculation, the person should be around 5 feet 5 inches in height. Even after four days, he could think in the same way he used to think earlier. A faint smile appeared on his lips, but soon vanished in the painful cracks that had developed due to his limited intake of water.

Until the second day, he could judge its four phases as well, despite the darkness around, but from the third day onward, he lost track. As of now, it was either day or night, difficult to judge, but then he heard some more footsteps.

From the sound of it, it became clear to him that there were three men coming his way. He had been lying in the corner, but on hearing someone arrive, he tried to pick his body up and tried to gain some decent position. He failed. He was too weak to move, but was happy because he wasn't too weak to think.

The rusted iron of the bars made an annoying sound when opened. The sound of those footsteps stopped.

“If your experiment is now over, can you please look after yourself? You look pathetic. Four days without anything. Why are you punishing yourself?” Inspector Naveen asked the man lying on the ground in the severe condition.

“My experiment is the only source of proving what can never be proved. A lie of a criminal,” he answered in his wavering voice.

“So how long then?” The Inspector sounded annoyed.

“Fifty-six steps for sunlight and around three minutes to food if the canteen is ready with the evening's meal.” He smiled. The Inspector ordered his other two companions to lift the man up.

“Sir, the murderer is the father himself. All the evidence is against him, and while I was in the cell, a strange hypothesis took me off guard.” The Chief investigating officer Raunak Upadhyay stood in front of his seniors, explaining the infamous murder case where a father was accused of killing his own daughter. It was a high profile case and the media had created a havoc for the Ghaziabad Police. Raunak had been called to solve the case as he was believed to be the best.

"Please elaborate," asked one of the seniors.

"Because of all the evidence that were against the father, we took him under custody, and after 4 days of continuous interrogation in the worst conditions possible, he remained silent. I tried the same to check the working of the human brain and the results were surprising. You can survive those conditions without getting mad," Raunak explained and paused.

Everyone expected for something more, but Raunak stayed silent.

"Is that all? Should I write this in the file? Are you joking, Raunak?" The senior was getting impatient.

"No, Sir. I was actually explaining the outcome of my four days in prison. The hypothesis that I am about to tell came to my mind much before." He took another pause and this time he had a smile on his face. A smile of arrogance, a smile that said, "I knew you would fall into this trap."He continued, "When I visited the crime scene, I noticed the rope that strangled the daughter through the ceiling fan. That had the clue which proved that the father was responsible for the murder. If I was the investigator, I would not have suggested any post mortem." He stopped and looked straight to the one who was actually investigating the case. The post mortem report had stated that the death had happened much before she was hanged and that's how the police had known it was a murder and not suicide.

"What was in the rope?"

"The special bowline."

"What?"

"Bowline is a knot specially used by military personnels. They are trained to use special kind of knots when dealing with ropes etc. Only a military person can have the knowledge about the kind of knot that I saw in the rope," Raunak completed his explanation.

"And we all know who is a military person in the whole case." His senior left his chair and picked his cap while saying the words. "The Father himself." He had a winning smile over his face. Now he could just puke everything in front of media and get the lost glory back.

His alarm beeped at 7 A.M sharp, but he was already awake or in other words, he never slept. Alarm did wake him up, but only from the thoughts he had in his mind. *Time to have a coffee!* He picked up his Bluetooth headphone and started to play his favourite music. He went straight to the kitchen and started his daily routine. *Routine, the only thing he hated the most!*

Being the child of a politician, Raunak was expected to follow his father's footsteps, but he chose something different. Politics wasn't something he wanted to pursue. He wanted to have an exciting life and the life of crime gave him that. Routine was the only thing he wanted to run away from.

His stature in the police department increased with every case he solved. He loved finding answers to difficult puzzles. But soon, things started to change. Those puzzles failed to excite him anymore and the reason was that they were too easy. The more he solved, the more he understood that the criminal follows a rhythm and that rhythm was in his catch. He knew exactly where the criminal would fall into his trap. The overall excitement he longed for was missing and that bothered him day and night.

Raunak had nothing in life expect his puzzles. No family, no love, no hobby, no aspirations. He was the kind of person who sank deep in his own world with every passing day.

Once he had done preparing his coffee, he would sip it slowly while standing next to his window from where he could see the children playing cricket in the common park. *Memories!* The more he wanted to forget them the more it came back. He opened the drawer to the side of his bed and pulled out a coin. The half-burned coin. It was a special one and had many memories attached to it. It appeared similar on both sides but was not. The burns were so special that it had made both sides look similar.

Raunak kept staring at the coin and then kept returned it to the drawer when his mobile started to ring. It took him one stare at the caller ID to recognize that it was Showtime!

# 3

*They were having their supper. His father kept looking for a perfect moment to initiate the topic. It seemed that he was about to listen to something his father wanted told to him.*

*After finishing meal, his father nodded to let the servants know that it was time to take away the dishes and bring the towels. It was a huge mansion and his father owned all the wealth around.*

*He was around ten years old and things that happened around were way beyond his intelligence. He was upset but had no one to talk about the same with. He often remained silent and angry. He loved to read and stay away from the reality. His books were his escape.*

*"I want to talk about all this," his father said when the son decided to leave the room.*

*"But I don't," he replied curtly. Under normal*

*circumstances, he feared his father, but today, things had become a little different. He started to experience different emotions and being at such a young age, it was natural to get confused and react like he did now.*

*"But how long will you stay silent? You should understand that it was necessary. We had no other choice."*

*"Don't use 'we' because I have my own choices and no one can stop me from having my choices," he said and left for his room, leaving his father who bowed his head in guilt or maybe anger. Who knew?*

Not even in his wildest dream did Avnish Batra think that today's outing would become so horrible for Sandy. Sirens of police vehicles and numerous men made the whole scene look horrifying. But it was more the dead body covered in a white sheet, being carried by four policemen to the white ambulance, that troubled him.

Sandy looked fear-struck. He refused to speak. His face bore no expression at all. That was when the field officer who had been assigned the case came to Avnish.

"I know it's been terrible day for you and your son." The officer forwarded his hand to Avnish. "Myself Raunak Upadhyay. Sorry to make you wait for so long. We wanted to be sure that we don't skip any of the evidence before the body is being dispatched."

"I can understand, officer," Avnish replied with his

formal tone and serious expressions. He was worried for his son but was keeping everything calm.

"How's champ?" Raunak asked about Sunny.

"Still shocked. In the main city, you usually don't end up watching a dead body every day." Avnish chuckled on his sarcasm, trying to wave off the fear and the tension for some time.

"So who discovered the body?" Raunak changed the topic and came on the point.

"Him. We were out for fishing here. Reached at around 6:30 in the morning and this came up at around 7:30." Avnish had already talked about all this with many policemen earlier. He started to get irritated. He just wanted to go back to his house now.

"Do you recognize him?" Raunak showed him a photograph of the body.

"No. I don't," Avnish replied in earnest. "I have a request. Can you please let us go now? Sandy is not doing well. He needs medical care or at least he needs to be dragged away from here. You have all my details. Just let me know and I'll be there to answer everything you ask for, but for now, let me go," Avnish replied in urgency because now he had lost his composure. Raunak sensed that immediately. He accepted Avnish's request and let him go.

"Victim's name is Rajgopal Dutta and he used to

work as the sales assistant in Big Bazaar outlet of South Delhi," the constable reported to Raunak when he sat on his chair in his cabin. This case was given to Raunak because he loved to handle such crime scenes where the murderer seemed to have lost his mind and performed disgusting crimes. Raunak had a strange reputation in whole of the police department. He was never appointed officially for any case, but was asked to look into the cases by his fellow police officers and he happily accepted the offer. Despite this being an open secret, no one questioned anyone because Raunak was exceptionally good. Raunak was kind of a nomad in the police department.

After a little nod from Raunak, the constable began with the forensic report. "He must have died at around three in the night. He died because of too much loss of blood from his limb. He was alive when left in the lake. His limb was cut in the cottage near the lake with an axe and was dragged to the lake. He struggled for around three hours and then died." The constable stopped.

"Painful death. A long forgotten revenge or a work of a psycho?" Raunak kept on blabbering to himself while looking straight in constable eyes. Raunak bit his upper lip and then ordered, "I need the history of this Rajgopal...whatever. Bring me anything that could make him the prey of a painful death."

The constable ran out of the cabin to begin with his orders and at the same moment, another police officer, the regional one, came running to call Raunak.

"Raunak, we have got something."

"What?"

*"Let me tell you the incident from where a child's life changed. It was 1988, 31st August. Flora and fauna were abundant at that place – a beautiful treat for the eyes of a normal man living a normal life in an urban surrounding."*

The video started streaming over the 42 inch LED TV. Raunak looked at it with keen eyes. He could see the backside of the killer, but the victim was right in front of his eyes. The fear-stuck face of victim, listening to the story, had a lot to say. He never knew that the camera recorded everything, but the killer knew it. He had set the camera angle pretty nicely. The video quality was not good; it was a kind of cheap hidden camera recording. It was all planned and Raunak had guessed till now that the video must have been 'gifted' by the killer himself.

"When did it come?" Raunak asked the officer, which left the other officer in shock because he had never told about the arrival of video footage to Raunak.

"It came in a parcel containing CD with a hand note, 'Would you like to hear a story?'" the officer explained.

Raunak looked at the video, listened to the story, and rubbed his chin as if thinking something. His mind suggested different things, but one thought kept nagging at him.

*"Rajesh stood dumbstruck for a moment. He saw his master fall towards the furnace, but before he could*

*fall over it, he fell chest-first into an iron rod, which penetrated him. The master died in that moment."*

Then, all of a sudden, the video went blank. It was actually trimmed by a video editor. The killer didn't want to show anything more than the story. *The Story!*

Raunak came out of the cabin and ran towards the storage room where files of past cases and criminals were kept. He knew where to find what he was looking for. He scanned ten to fifteenfiles and then forwarded his hand towards the file he wanted to read. The front cover read 2002-03.

The file had a thin layer of dust accumulated over it, but Raunak didn't care to rub it off. He simply sat on the corner bench and opened the file to search for the case he was looking for. 'The Storyteller Murderer'. It was the fanciest case that media loved to publicize.

Raunak could never forget the case. It actually changed everything for him.

The killer was behind the bars after killing thirteen men and women. He had been caught while attempting his fourteenth kill. It had been the most sensational story of that time. The specialty of the killer was that he used to make his victim hear a story before he murdered them and used to record everything for the police and media to see. He used to send the clip direct to the media. He was a publicity seeker.

Raunak wondered whether someone was following the same trend. Thankfully, the media wasn't involved this time. *But for how long?*

# 4

"Listen...... listen to me once atleast for God's sake. I saved your life, I helped you that day, and you are doing this to me. Please, for God's sake, let me go." His prey trembled a lot while he spoke, but the firmness in voice never faded. Perhaps, his work place's fake confidence had now have become a part of his life and that part was still active.

*Even in the darkest hour, have faith in light.* He remembered his father's words while he observed the fear-struck prey of his. He roamed all over the basement, pretending to find something, but in reality, he enjoyed his prey's blabbering. *Danger pulls out your inner self.* 'It is better to know the person who you are about to kill,' he thought and smiled.

Finally, the blabbering stopped and the sobbing started. That's the part he didn't like. He picked up his favourite axe and a chair and adjusted it opposite his prey. He sat upon it and stared straight into the eyes of his prey.

"Do you want to hear a story?"

"Story? Are you insane? You bought me here for a story?" The blabbering came back, though it wasn't out of fear. More of confusion, he would say.

"The thing for which I have bought you here will surely come up as well, but for that you have to wait and just tell me one thing." he took a dramatic pause and then began, "Do you have any choice other than to listen?" His voice was firm, deep and frightening, but his face was gentle. He never appeared as if he could really harm anyone. He was a kind of 'illusion' for his prey.

"Let's begin!"

*The year was 1988 and the date... date can be assumed as any one of the first five days of September. He was nine-year- old when he escaped the 'jail'.*

*After almost a day of walking the roads, not knowing where to go or what to do, he found a truck whose driver was pissing near the bushes. Sahab was the name of the truck's driver and Chotu Bhaiya was the helper. He requested Sahab for some food, which Sahab gave. Chotu Bhaiya enquired about whereabouts of the child. He told everything. Chotu Bhaiya requested Sahab to take the child on board. Sahab agreed.*

*For the first time, he was happy. He thought his days would change. He was having his first experience of any kind of vehicle. He had a broad smile over his face. The world was bigger than he had imagined.*

*Sahab never talked. He preferred to stay silent while Chotu Bhaiya was a complete opposite. Chotu and the child were having a good time. The child could see in Chotu Bhaiya a brother, a friend.*

*The sun lowered down and the fun time soon became one of frustration. Too much of hard roads meant a hard time to the child. He wasn't so good with travelling. His stomach and head ached, but he remained silent. The pain became unbearable so he decided to tell Chotu Bhaiya about it. Fine lines of tension appeared on Chotu's forehead as he knew the child was in trouble. Chotu could see that the child was in pain, but he knew what would happen if the news reached Sahab's ears. Chotu started to ignore the child in a hope to escape the situation.*

*At around midnight, Sahab took a halt for dinner and that's when Chotu decided to confront the situation by telling everything to Sahab. The child witnessed the conversation from a distance, but couldn't hear anything except a tight slap that Sahab gave Chotu on the latter's face. Chotu lowered his head when he noticed that the child had seen everything. Sahab decided to leave everyone for his dinner at the highway-side dhaba.*

*A few silent moments passed between Chotu and the child, but then a loud moan of pain escaped the child's mouth. That evoked Chotu's anger.*

*"Is it paining badly?" Chotu asked the child. He searched for something at the back of his trouser while asking the question.*

*The child stayed silent for the moment.*

*"I asked you something. Answer me." Chotu finally found what he was looking for. A knife he always kept for safety.*

*The child nodded in pain and at that moment, Chotu took one of the child's hands and forcefully expanded it over the nearby wall to pierce the knife. The child shouted in pain, but Chotu covered his scream by putting another over his mouth.*

*"Now tell me, what is paining more badly? Your head, stomach or your palm?"*

"Same terror. I can see that same terror in your eyes. Your eyes are reflecting that child's terror, but why?" He picked up the axe and stood up. His prey looked terrified to speak anything. "How was the story? Tragic? Sad? Abrupt?" He paused and scanned his prey and loved the feel of fear.

"Why are you afraid? I haven't yet started." He picked the axe up and lowered it with force over his left limb and made a deep cut. Flood started flowing out, and after a few moments, a loud scream escaped from his prey's throat. *Such a bliss.* "Now, you should start fearing as this was just a start."

# 5

Raunak gave a loud sigh before entering the gate that read, in bold letters, Jasmit Singh - Commissioner of Police. Raunak knew how badly Jasmit hated to work with him, but eventually, every now and then, they had to cross each other's paths.

Raunak entered, saluted, and waited for Jasmit Singh signal to seat. A while later, it came and Raunak sat opposite to the commissioner.

Jasmit sat watching something on his laptop. Raunak could only hear the man speaking. “The future lies in the hands of science. 'What we can't do' has become the question that you should not ask any of the scientists around. They asked me how can we help the criminals to treat their thoughts and push them towards the normal life. I presented them the solution, a dream simulator.” Jasmit reversed the screen towards Raunak. He was watching Ted talks of some scientist.

“Dr. Virendra Tripathy. They wanted to use these

dream simulators in our prisons as well, but I thought we should wait and test the consequences before taking such a huge step." Jasmit said. Raunak turned the screen again towards Jasmit to tell him that he wasn't interested to hear more about it.

"So you think that someone is trying to draw everyone's attention towards him by following the trend of...... what was his name?" Jasmit looked at the file kept on the table by adjusting his spectacles a bit. "Dharmendra Nath, also known as Storyteller murderer." He took a pause as he wanted to hear from Raunak.

"I don't think so. He is not behind publicity, but is trying to prove a point," Raunak replied quickly.

"What point?"

"No idea." Another quick and straight reply. That followed by a silence.

"Why is he making videos if he is not behind publicity?" Another question from Jasmit.

"If he needed publicity, he would have approached media, not the police. Just the way our 'story-teller' did."

"Maybe he was afraid of being caught?" The Commissioner regretted saying those words. Raunak smiled a bit, but then stopped.

"He is sending videos directly to the police. That's more of a difficult task." He took a pause and then came directly to the point. "I want permission to meet Nath. I think I can have some leads from there."

"Isn't it a bit early to think that there's any kind of connection between Nath and our murderer?"

Commissioner Jasmit heard the landline ringing and picked it up while he talked to Raunak. He answered the call. "Shit! When?" He paused. His forehead began to sport the fine lines of tension Raunak was familiar with. He put the receiver down.

"We got another video. He killed again." He stood up and forwarded towards the door and thought that Raunak would follow with the same urgency.

"Sir, I'll examine the video later. I want your permission first." Jasmit nodded and left Raunak.

South Delhi had always been full of life, but every time Naveen visited here, he'd always been on a murder case. He entered the mall and directly visited the manager of the Big Bazaar. Naveen was in uniform and as always faced a similar reaction. The manager left his seat to greet the inspector and then both sat on the opposite side of the only table resting in the small cabin.

"Tell me something about…" Naveen struggled to remember the name for few seconds, but soon recalled, "Rajgopal Dutta."

Naveen waited to see the reaction of the manager. The manager said nothing in a go. Naveen then elaborated his question, "I mean his behaviour with colleagues, anyone who could have any motive behind killing him like this, his background, anything that you can remember about him?"

"Rajgopal…. He was just like everyone else.

Normal kind of a guy… he was rebellious sometimes regarding salary hike and all, but then he had some problems at the home as well, maybe with the mother and all…. So never tried to leave the job. I don't think anyone can have any motive to kill him or anything like that." The manager was perspiring, stammering in between as well. Suddenly, the manager called a guy named Piyush.

"Sir, he is Piyush. He's a good friend of Rajgopal. He can help you with some insight about the murder."

Naveen stood up from the chair and looked at Piyush from top to bottom, and then asked, "How do you know Rajgopal?"

"We…we work here together. I am also a sales executive just like him. Also, he lived in my neighbourhood. We often meet at night over…" He stopped a bit, then continued, "over meetings." He meant to say over drinking sessions. Naveen understood that and didn't ask anything further about the same.

"Was he in debt or something? Or in some business that could result in his death?" Naveen asked.

"No, Sir. He was a pure guy just like me. We earn from what we do here, Sir. No extra income, Sir. Very pure, Sir," Piyush replied in a hurry.

"Then why would someone kill him so brutally?" Naveen asked by raising his voice. Everyone around froze for a moment.

"I don't know, Sir." Piyush started sobbing.

Naveen grew irritated. "Tell me everything about this guy or every one of you will come with me, understood?" Naveen shouted at the top of his voice. Some customers out at the billing counter even heard him shouting.

"Sir... please, Sir, I am telling you everything. You first please have a seat." The manager insisted, but Naveen was unmoved. He wanted to hear the story.

"Three days ago, one customer came to us. Rajgopal attended him. He bought clothes for Rs. 3000, and during billing, he told us that he forgot to bring his purse in the car. According to our procedure, in this case, we simply leave the customer, but Rajgopal was in good mood or I don't know what the reason was. Rajgopal paid for him and walked towards the customer's car to fetch the money. The customer paid the amount and Rajgopal returned." The manager told the story in a complete monotonous way. "The real problem began the next day. Rajgopal came to me and said that he thought that the customer was stalking him. I ignored his words because why would a customer, 'male' customer follow a 'male' sales executive. I told him he must be mistaken. But he kept on begging for people's attention. He even claimed that the customer even came inside his house without anyone noticing. Next day, we heard that his body was found in the lake."

Naveen waited to hear more of it, but nothing came from anybody. It was all absurd. "Do anyone of you know who the customer was?"

"No. We did some internal research as well because we knew we had to answer at some time or another."

"Soon a sketch artist will come. I want you all to help him." Naveen said and left the premises to call Raunak and inform him about the developments.

It was not the first time that Raunak had chosen to follow a different path to solve the case. He believed in his gut feeling. He had a positive vibe that this visit with Dharmendra Nath will clear some dust out of the case.

Raunak was in his vehicle, travelling towards the Central Jail when his phone buzzed. The caller identified himself as Naveen, who wanted to inform Raunak about the strange story of the victim. Raunak was nearby to Naveen's location so he thought to simply pick him up and take him on the visit.

The moment Naveen saw Raunak in the parking lot observing something keenly, he forgot the case and asked Raunak what the thing was that grabbed his attention. Raunak continued looking in the direction of a car with half-open black glasses. Soon, a hand came out with a cigarette to clear off the ashes. Naveen found nothing interesting but Raunak's eye was fixed on the car.

"What?" Naveen asked while taking the seat.

"That Cigar, Cohiba Behike. Exclusively made in Cuba. Do you know the price?" Raunak asked.

"No."

"Well, don't even try to guess," Raunak said and steered out of the parking lot. Whenever Naveen thought that he had seen enough of Raunak, Raunak introduced something new in style.

On the way, when Naveen explained the story to

Raunak, contrary to Naveen's assumption, Raunak showed no surprise. Raunak was thinking on some parallel level.

Soon, they reached their destination, completed the formalities, and proceeded towards the common ground where, at the far end, on a bench, an old man sat quietly. The recreational hours were on. During these hours, all the prisoners were taken out of their cells to take fresh air. The prisoners loved these few hours of the day, but the old man seemed to be busy running in his own thoughts.

The first detail about the old man was his long, white, disoriented beard. Those dust wrangled, yellowish cloths with black trips running all over and the white beard, gave this old man a kind of eerie presence.

There was complete silence between all the three when Naveen decided to break it. "Dharmendra Nath. We want to talk."

"He is not here," the old man replied in harsh and faint voice. "I think you have mistaken. I am prisoner no. 23. They call me by this name." He was still looking down at the ground. But finally, he decided to look up at the face of the stranger with whom he was talking.

The old man showed no response when he saw the face of Naveen, but when his eyes fell on Raunak, his expressions changed drastically. At first, he showed surprise, and then there was a glimpse of anger, and finally a smile. "I knew you would come back to see me." The old man started to laugh and behave in the most childish manner. Naveen was stunned to hear Dharmendra's words. 'Come back? They have met earlier before?' Naveen thought. Raunak was caught off

guard to hear the old man's words. He knew what Naveen was thinking and at the very moment, Raunak landed a tight slap on the old man's face.

Everyone around froze for a second. That was totally unexpected. The old man was believed to be mentally ill. No one ever behaved in such a manner with him. The old man was on the ground, crying. Raunak bent his knee to get a grip of old man's collar when he whispered in Raunak's ear, "Sir, please not here. Let's go behind that tree. I'll tell you everything there only. Please, sir."

Raunak agreed. Naveen was still clueless about what was happening. The moment the three of them were veiled behind the tree, the old man's way of talking changed drastically. "Sir, please don't tell anyone."

"Why are you faking then?" Raunak asked while grabbing the old man's collar.

"Sir, they used to beat me a lot. Since the day I am doing this acting of talking in loops and forgetting everything, they have left me on my own. If they got to know I was faking about my mental condition, they'll start beating me again. Please, sir…."

"Someone has just killed a guy, filmed it in the same manner you used to film. Do you know anything about it?" Raunak directly came to the point. Naveen was still confused but didn't interrupt the investigation. "If you know anything and you try to hide, I'll make sure that this place becomes hell for you."

"That means he was actually serious?" the old man responded with surprise.

"Tell me about it," Raunak demanded.

"Sir, he was my cell-mate here. The day you came, he heard you, and after hearing your words, he said, don't worry, I'll make sure he enjoys every bit of it." The old man took a pause. There were so many puzzles in the story. "He told me his plan that after escaping from here, he'll play with you the same game and make sure you'll have fun."

Raunak's forehead started to shrink.

# 6

They had already seen the video umpteenth of times but wanted to see it once more to grasp all the details. The aura of the cabin naturally changed to its worst when the commissioner of police seems to be off mood. He had the most important meeting that could have changed the way we deal with criminals, but he had to cancel everything and sit to watch another criminal's deed. Lights were off; the screen of a 42-inch display plasma television was adjusting with some signal issues. Everyone knew that the days were going to be tough because in a city like Delhi, where safety and security is already a really big issue, handling a serial killer's case was nothing more than a nightmare.

“The year was 1988 and the date… date can be assumed as any one of the first 5 days of September. He was 9 years old when he escaped the 'jail'……”

The video was similar to the last one. The delivery pattern was the same and the story seemed to be in

continuation. Everyone heard every detail with full attention. No one wanted to miss anything. The story-telling was impressive. The voice of the man narrating the story had an amazing power of grasping the audience.

"Now tell me, what is paining more badly? Your head, stomach or your palm?" The video ended abruptly just like the previous one, but this time, there were few lines written at the end as well.

'A Few minutes later, Sahab and Chotu died in an accident. The child escaped.'

Lights were back again. Everyone was looking at the commissioner's face but he was looking at the figure standing next to the gate, Raunak Upadhyay.

Before commissioner could ask about Raunak's view over the video, as he always did, Raunak himself started narrating his hypothesis.

"A few things are now clarified about the murderer. First, he will kill more. Second, he wants to tell a story and this story is the only thing which can help us reach him before he makes his next move. Third, he himself wants us to get him. He is giving us clues. The year 1988 and the last line describing the accident is our clue." He stopped for a while. Everyone thought he'd done with his hypothesis, so started thinking about it, but then again Raunak started, "One more thing, the video is edited by free software. See the watermark at the bottom of the screen, Viva-Movies.com. We can track his location through this website."

Jasmit Singh instantly began his follow-up. "Call the cyber cell. Get them to work and find everything about this video. Send them one copy of it,

immediately." He moved to another inspector and instructed, "Search all the major, minor accidents happened in 1988 in which the truck is involved. Get as many men as you want, but get me the information within the next twelve hours." Jasmit was thinking something and suddenly turned towards Raunak, "and lastly, you, Raunak, come to my office immediately."

"What happened with Dharmendra Nath? What's all this about 'second meet' with him?" Instantly, Raunak realized the Naveen has leaked all the information to Jasmit. Raunak had no other option but to tell him the truth.

"I met Dharmendra Nath before as well, just after the court gave the verdict on him. I wanted to thank him." Raunak was interrupted in midway.

"Thank him? For what?" Jasmit asked in surprise.

"For giving me the case that I deserved. I loved solving the puzzle that he made for me. Those few months were the best experience for me." Raunak had a spark in his eyes. Jasmit had an idea about the abnormal behaviour of Raunak -- in fact, everyone had -- but because of his brilliance, no one said or questioned anything. Jasmit decided to keep his silence as well.

"So what's the outcome of your visit?" Jasmit asked while lying back on his chair.

"Some idiotic, psychopath heard my conversation with Dharmendra, and now in his overconfidence,

wants to play with me. But, don't worry, I'll catch the bastard soon." Raunak replied in a firm voice. Instantly, Raunak's right hand slipped into his right pocket of the trouser. He touched the coin and started rubbing it. It was the coin that always reminds him of his past; past that he wanted to forget but couldn't.

"You mean to say, everything that is happening around is because of you?" Jasmit came forward over the table resting in between Raunak and him.

"Not completely. We only know the half of the story. The other half lies in his version of the story that he wants us to know," Raunak replied.

"Listen, Raunak. If this case goes out of control, you'll be the person who'll take the responsibility of all these killings."

Raunak rose from his chair and said nothing. He simply saluted the commissioner of the police and left. He pulled out the half-burnt coin out of his pocket and flipped it in the air just to catch it back.

*"We are born same but the rules of game for everyone of us were different. For some the struggles were in finding the food, for others, struggles were related to how to excel and for some there were no struggles at all. Everyone on different level but then what makes us the same? What is that one thing that defines us? What is that one thing that keeps us moving?" His father was looking at his face curiously*

*while talking. He could feel the trembling thoughts of his son while watching the change in expressions over his face. He indeed loved his son and the sole motive of it was that he was a good student and one thing that the father loved was teaching. He loved to teach life but before his son, no one heard him so attentively. Now as he had audience, he loved to do what he loves the most.*

*"That one thing, my son, is that every one of us, if having a pain within us. Suffering is life and suffering is the only thing that keeps us moving. We suffer and in hope of getting it eradicated from our life, we run, we run places just to find the peace but what we get, is more suffering. That's what life is!"*

There wasn't even a single day when he hadn't admired the lessons of his father. His father is the only figure that had shaped the course of his life. He helped him in giving the answers of the most complicated things that happened with him at early teenage; the age at which other children play among themselves, he was playing with life and death and witnessing the cruel world with open eyes.

The day was normal. Birds chirping all around, smooth and cold wind blowing and making the trees dance around and faint voices from the basement. Still crying? He thought but then switched his thought process immediately. He needed to hear the news to get the idea of what is happening in the world but before that, he needed to make breakfast for his captive. So without wasting any time, he switched on his radio and went straight to the kitchen. Once the breakfast was ready, he slowly descended the stairs and reached to the basement.

The captive realized the company and instantly

started to initiate the conversation.

"Listen, please leave me. I know who you are." The man bound with ropes on a chair said and that made the other man lose his control over the breakfast plate that he was holding. Instantly he started thinking, how the hell can he know me?

"I saw the photo of your father lying at the table above. I know you want to take revenge of what I did while defending your case. I am sorry but I had no other option." The man cried. He was a lawyer by profession and assuming all this to be the result of one of his cases that he fought many years ago.

The man with the plate in his hand now felt relaxed and simply kept the plate on the table lying nearby. He smiled and said, "We always try to solve the puzzle in the quickest way possible but forget one important rule. Here, time is not an issue but you have to be very accurate with what you say, do or act." He left the food on the table and started leaving when the man tied with ropes shouted, "How am I supposed to eat the food?"

"I suppose your mouth is still untied." He said and left.

# 7

Raunak paid no attention to the commissioner's warning because his mind was occupied with the details of the case. Threats, warnings, consequences -- these were the few things that came to his mind at the very end of the thought lane. The moment he left the commissioner's office, he rushed towards his own cabin to delve himself into the file that he had got from the central jail on the prisoner Dharmendra talked about. On his way towards the cabin, he saw a Constable yawning over the chair. The moment their eyes met, the constable jumped out of his chair and saluted Raunak.

"Bring two cups of tea. Quick. Give one to me, treat yourself to another one," Raunak said in a loud and firm voice that made constable shiver for a second.

The moment he reached inside his own cabin, he saw the disordered files over the table. He paid no heed to settle them up. Just with a single swing of his arm, he

threw everything on the floor to make way for the new file. He sat in his chair, straightened his back, and puffed a long breath before turning his thoughts to the file.

The first thing about the file that grabbed the attention of Raunak was the childish face of the person. By no means had he looked dangerous.

Name: Sudhir Nagpal, Age: 35. This meant that his current age would be around thirty-eight as the file was documented three years ago. He had been caught numerous times before. Raunak read about everything. Where he was born, what he did in his childhood, his studies, his cases, charges, each and every detail. In the meanwhile, the constable brought him a cup of tea as well, but Raunak paid no attention. Something struck the cords of the brain of Raunak while reading the file and he needed access to the record room for clarification. He did not waste a single second and marched towards the record room. Raunak was a frequent visitor there and hence no one asked him any question. He picked up some old files from different years. It was as if he knew what he was searching for. Hours passed, but his enthusiasm was still the same, and then finally, he came to a conclusion. He came out of the record room and rushed towards the Commissioner's Office. He wanted to let him know about his findings, but he was not in the cabin. In fact, almost half of the department was empty. Raunak decided to call the commissioner and he did.

"Hello." In a sleepy voice, Jasmit replied.

"Sir, this case is something fishy. All the records...." Raunak was filled with assumptions about the case and wanted to pour them down in a single go,

but Jasmit interrupted.

“It's 2 past midnight, Raunak. Grab some sleep. We'll discuss it in the morning.” Jasmit cut the phone line and slept again. He was not annoyed because he knew Raunak very well.

Raunak then realized that he had spent really long hours in the record room. He decided to call it a day when the same constable arrived with a sketch.

“Sir, Naveen Sir told me to give this sketch to you. The staff at Big Bazaar helped to make this one.”

“The same childish face,” Raunak said to himself and chuckled. He knew that the killer was now not so far away from his grab.

Raunak roared back to his apartment as the city was getting ready to recognize the killer they were breeding all along. Posters of the sketch were distributed all around; the only wait was of the rising of the sun.

“Leaving so late?” The clock was showing 2 hours past midnight when one of his colleagues noticed him leaving the premises of the call centre where he worked.

“Actually needed to clear my account. The HR thing.” He chuckled and kept on moving, showing the urgency.

“See you tomorrow,” the colleague said to which

he simply smiled. 'You'll never see me again, mate,' he thought.

He did not waste a single moment because he knew he had limited time, although he was not in a hurry as everything was going according to the plan. He drove straight towards the place where he knew he can fetch the things he needed in those wee hours.

Once he reached, he knocked the iron shutter as the shop was closed. No response, he now knocked it with more strength. A faint voice greeted him from inside.

"Coming. Wait!" The shop owner whispered from inside. Slowly, he lifted the shutter, trying to make a minimum noise.

"Sudhir Bhai, what's the urgency? You could have come in the morning. Spoiled the whole night." The man paid no attention to the words of the shop owner, simply gave him the list of items he wanted and some cash. The shop owner could easily see that the money was way more than the items will cost and hence got on the work quietly, but immediately. The shop had all the items of daily need and that's what he actually wanted. The shop owner took around twenty minutes to pack everything from the list, and after that, he helped the man to keep everything in his car, but before he started the engine, the shop owner again asked out of curiosity, "Are you going somewhere out for a week?"

"Go and grab some sleep. Tomorrow will be a busy day for you." The shop owner understood nothing. He was confused, but then he saw the money he got for the deal. Compensating.

The sky was now turning dark blue, the morning was about to arrive. Soon this city would recognize the man who rode in the 'early hours' and enjoying the morning breeze. Everything was planned and that was the beauty of this day.

*"Do you know son what's the one thing that everyone wants to have but everyone will hate once they have?" His father asked. Son, as usual, stayed silent. Father knew that the son had no answer, and hence continued, "The ability to see the future." The father replied to his own question and then took a gap before explaining his point, "The future is depressing, present is full of hopes, and hope requires hard work. But if you can see the future and look at the outcome of your hard work, it will spoil your soul because in this world, nothing goes according to plan. I would say, planning is the only stupidity that a person can do again and again and again."*

That's the only memory of his father to which he denied. He admired his father for his philosophy, but this particular thing is absurd. Planning was necessary and this gave up the strength and the confidence to face the future.

Soon, he reached the spot from where he needed to change the vehicle and move forward to his favourite place, his playground.

Finally, he was home and, as usual, no one greeted him. The abandoned warehouse in the middle of the jungle where even the wild animals don't wander, this was indeed heaven for this man. He arranged the entire ration he collected in a proper manner. That took him a couple of hours but now time was not limited as from now till the next one week; he is having plenty of time.

He prepared the breakfast and while doing so he realized that his captive must be starving. He heard nothing from him so far. He hurried to the breakfast and descended towards the basement. The man was still tied with the plastic chair with ropes, but was on the floor. The struggle he had for hours was visible all over the floor. He was asleep at that moment but when a few drops of water fell on his face, he regained consciousness. The man helped the captive to eat as he seemed to have no power to struggle further.

The man waited for the perfect moment to start because he wanted the captive to be in his full senses when it all began. Till that time, he adjusted the camera angle. He changed it now as the face was not an issue. They already had the photograph so there wasn't a point to stay anonymous. He created the whole environment and the captive kept on watching it all happening around him. Maybe he had the idea that this meal would have been his last but this time he wasn't panicking because maybe last few hours have shown him the worst.

“Why me?” The captive finally, out of curiosity

asked the question for which the man was not ready.

"Because you had some questions and I never like to leave the questions, unanswered." The man replied.

"Are doing all this out of revenge? First, you took revenge on your father and now you are doing it with me? But you do know I had no choice." The captive was whispering out of pain.

"Revenge is not in my dictionary. As I said, I am just answering your questions," answered the man with no emotion on his face.

"What questions are you talking about?"

The man stayed silent to which his prey only nodded. He knew what to expect.

"So how will you do it?" Finally, the captive surrendered to his fate but had no clue what was planned for him.

"By telling you a story."

# 8

*The year was 1988, somewhere in the mid of September, when he met the two most important people in his life. The year indeed was full of events for him and hence, he was ready for anything. He was wandering the streets when he heard something from behind the long bushes. The night was at its darkest hour and not a single soul could be seen anywhere in the vicinity. He could see the continuous blinking of lights from a vehicle that was parked at the side of the road. As he moved forward, the voice grew louder but the voice wasn't coming from the car, it was coming from the bushes.*

*'The voice belongs to a female and must have her mouth shut by a cloth or so', he thought. He picked up a stone that could fit in his fist and forwarded towards the voice. He had no idea what he'll do but gut feeling made him do that stupid thing. Suddenly the voice stopped and that made him stop as well. He saw a man standing*

*in the bushes, buttoning his shirt. His hairs were disoriented and he was panting heavily. He had a huge smile on his face. He was talking to someone who was still lying on the ground. The child could see everything as the man was standing just below the street light. Soon he took out his purse and gave a lot of money to the other person who was on the ground. That was the time when his eyes fell on the child standing with a stone in his hand. The child should have run away but something made him stay. The man came in rushing towards him, abusing him. The child sensed the danger and out of simple reflex action, he threw the stone on the man's forehead. The man fell to the ground instantly, fainted.*

*After all this, she came out of the bushes, handling her naked body and few clothes. She was not shy about coming out of those bushes in such a state; it was not the first time for her to be running without clothes at those hours on the lonely road. Her eyes had fear, but not panic. The child's eyes had none. He was firm, she was surprised. She lay down in front of the unconscious man; she instantly found that the man had died. She stood up, looked the child from head to toe asked him about whereabouts, he replied in his full story. While listening, she adjusted her clothes and then held the child's hand and took him directly to where she belonged; the red light area.*

*The place was incredible. For the first time, the child saw naked man and woman, not just by clothes, but by their nature. Human behaviour was as pure as it should be. The city may have been sleeping but this place was full of activity. The child was looking everywhere as if the Alice had come from her wonderland. But the most important part of all this was*

*the lady that held the child's hand. The authority that she had shown over the child was just like a mother showed in hers. The child, for the very first time in years, felt the motherhood.*

*She instructed the child to stay at a specific place till she returns. They were on the fourth floor. She went inside a room and then came out with a man who looked big and powerful. He was wearing a white kurta and was looking at the boy with disgust. The lady was continuously begging for something and finally, the man agreed.*

*She came back to the child, embraced his hair, and kissed his forehead. For the child, this kind of affection was strange. Suddenly, everyone around started to shout. People started running out from different rooms and buildings. The lady looked terrified. She ran into the same room where that man was staying. This time she took the child with her. She told everything that's happening outside and that made the man stand and panic in fear. A few policemen entered the room and at the very moment, the man held the child's hand and pushed the lady out of the window from where she fell down on the ground floor and died.* "What kind of story was that?"

"That's what I ask regularly, but no one answered it yet," that childish face replied. His prey still waited for some sense to come up in what was happening with him, but it seemed to him that there was no end to this madness.

The dawn had come. A thought ran through the hunter's mind and he whispered to himself, "Here begins the game."

Raunak was all charged up, sitting in his cabin when he saw that Jasmit, the commissioner, has just arrived at the police station. Jasmit called Raunak instantly to his cabin as he knew that Raunak had been waiting for long. He was surprised to see the energy of a person who must have slept barely for a couple of hours the previous night.

"Sir, this person, who is our suspect, is a much bigger player than we think. There's something interesting about his background." Raunak started while taking the chair opposite to the Jasmit. There was no one in the cabin, just the two of them. Raunak forwarded the file that had all the information he had gotten from the central jail about the suspect.

"Sudhir Nagpal…." Jasmit read the first page of the file and instantly Raunak interrupted.

"I doubt that's the real name of this person." Instantly, Jasmit kept the file back on the table and leaned back to listen to the theory that Raunak had worked upon.

"Everything that's written in this file is a lie and I can prove it to you if you give me ten more minutes of yours." Raunak was building the aura.

"I am all ears, Inspector."

"This file in front of you has all the details of this man whom we know as Sudhir Nagpal. Now I want you to look at the hospital where he was born, the first report against him, every single judge he had faced in his life's

trials, just look at them and see the pattern," Raunak said.

Jasmit waited for more but then realized that Raunak wanted him to open the file and look by himself. He did the same, read the entire name. Nothing struck at him. He looked at Raunak again and said, "Come to the point."

"The hospital mentioned got burned in 1992, the first report against him was in some remote area of Chattisgarh, that too caught up in the fire in the same year, and the judges mentioned, all are dead now. So my point is, who-so-ever has made this file, he knew a great deal about the system and is aware of how to make fools of us. There's not a single place left from where we can trace this man. This man must have done something terrible, or my gut feeling says, he will do something terrible." Raunak rested on the chair and Jasmit was all confused, looking at the files once again in the hope of finding something that Raunak had mentioned.

"But... how can we be so sure that we are finding this man only and we are not mistaken? There could be a chance that we are mixing two very different cases here," Jasmit said.

"No chance, Sir. The staff at the mall where the victim number 1 was working made one sketch and that sketch matches the photo on this file. Even if we ignore this detail, there's one more thing. Read the name of the jailer he had in current jail."

"Armaan Malik. He is our...." Jasmit was about to say something, but Raunak interrupted and completed the sentence.

"Armaan Malik is the second victim of our killer."

Raunak, after his visit to the commissioner's office, called Naveen inside his cabin and took the report of all the posters that they had put over the entire city.

"We have received seventeen calls from anonymous sources and almost all of them talk about the call centre at Noida. I have dispatched one team to the specified place and we are waiting for the initial report." Naveen gave the brief, but Raunak left his chair in an instant.

"Let's move, we don't have that much time left. I suspect, we'll receive the third tape today only."

The moment Raunak and Naveen came out of the police station, their eyes fell on the enormous crowd of media. They saw Jasmit giving a statement about the double murder to the media and filling their ears with what they already knew. Raunak hated the media, but they seemed to love him. The moment media saw him coming out they gathered around him and started questioning. Raunak was famous for being blunt and creating sensation throughout the city. He was never politically correct and that's what Jasmit feared.

"Sir, who this murderer is and are we safe on the streets when such a murderer is roaming among us?"

"Nobody is safe in this city as this city is full of criminals. Now, let us do work as he is on the hunt at this very moment as well. He is ready with his sharp knife or whatever he likes and send us a video again." Raunak pushed the media away and sat on the jeep with Naveen to the call centre.

Jasmit cursed Raunak under his breath for disclosing the video thing in front of the media. Now he was not ready to answer the new sets of questions so he quietly left, leaving media to guess and report whatever they felt like.

# 9

"Sir, yesterday only he cleared his account, as he said, he'll leave the town in the morning as his mother is ill. He kept me working until midnight for the stuff. I had no idea that...." The accountant at the call centre replied to the same question for the third time. This time it was to Raunak and Naveen as they wanted to hear everything again.

"When did he join this call centre?" Raunak bombarded his question on everyone. They had gathered in a room -- all who were somehow connected to Sudhir.

"6 months ago."

"Did you know about his criminal background?"

"Yes, he disclosed everything about himself. We thought that the person is genuine and hence we had no other thought."

"How was his behaviour?"

"Pretty normal. He loved to work. Not a single leave was taken during his tenure. He didn't like to talk to anyone. Always quiet."

"Any particular place where he liked to visit often?"

Everyone looked at each other. One of them answered, "Sir, there's a shop at the crossing, of daily needs. That's the only place I have seen him quite often, and even last night, he went in that direction."

Raunak looked at Naveen. Raunak understood that the murderer knew about all this and hence had made himself ready. He must have bought ration for next few days and had gone underground.

Raunak asked a few more questions, recorded the statements, and then left to the daily needs shop. The moment he reached the shop, he noticed few things which confirmed his doubt that the night was long for the shopkeeper. The newspaper was still lying on the ground. No one picked it up. The milk packets still lay unattended and the shopkeeper looked totally disoriented, all suggesting that the person just got up.

"What's your closing time?"

"10 at night."

"And last night, why were you open till 2?" Naveen guessed the time, and by the shopkeeper's sudden reaction, he knew that he had hit the bull's eye.

"No, Sir, I… I haven't." Raunak slapped him on his face and within a second he started puking everything he knew.

"Sir Sudhir Bhai told me to wait till 2 as he would be coming to gather some stuff and he is my regular

client, I couldn't deny. He even gave me some really good tip."

"How much?"

"Around two thousand"

"And what was the cost of the stuff he bought?"

"Eight thousand."

"Hm... means around 1 week's stuff. Vehicle?"

"He came on an Alto, red color. I remember the number of the car as well. 7466."

Raunak smiled. Just one slap and the person became a parrot. Raunak slipped his hand into his right pocket of trouser and turned the coin. It was his habit to constantly touch the coin and turn it or flip it in the air to catch it back.

It didn't take long to trace the vehicle. They got the location within half an hour and without wasting even a single minute they proceeded towards it. The location was far away from the city and it took around one and a half hour to reach the location. During this time, Naveen couldn't hide his curiosity to ask about the coin. Raunak loved to flip that coin within his fingers whenever he was thinking about something. The coin was pretty special too. It was half burnt on both the sides.

"Is that your lucky charm? That coin?" Naveen asked.

Raunak chuckled on hearing it because that coin could be anything but a lucky charm. “This coin is a symbol. It reminds me of that one case that still remains unsolved. I keep this with me as a reminder that how badly an unsolved case hurts.”

“Unsolved case? As far as I know, Sir, you have a track record of 100%. I can't remember any unsolved case of yours.”

“Some things in life are way too personal, Naveen, and this case is among them only,” Raunak said and Naveen realised that he must have hit some personal cord. He fell silent and stayed so until they reached their destination.

On the NH-44, at a place where you least expected to stop, among the long bushes, they found the red Alto with the number plate 7466. Raunak had a bad feeling about the whole scenario from the very beginning. He knew that the murderer was way too intelligent than running on a car with a number plate.

“The suspect has deliberately left his car over here and has changed the vehicle from here." Raunak went a little inside the bushes to have a look at the surroundings. For the first time, he felt his heart running at a rapid speed. For the first time, he felt the fear. He picked out the coin from his pocket and bit it between his teethes and that's when he heard Naveen shouting his name.

“We have found something here. A new set of tire imprints. We are tracing it and soon will get the details of the vehicle.”

Raunak inspected the tire imprint and wasn't convinced to get any information from them. Naveen looked keenly when Raunak was observing the tire imprint.

“What happened?” Naveen asked.

“The depth.”

“The what?”

“These imprints are of a heavy vehicle, but the depth suggests the vehicle was lighter one. He recently had changed the tires of the vehicle that he is using.” Raunak replied.

“What's the conclusion, then?”

“You'll get nothing from these imprints. We are following a master here,” Raunak said and left the vicinity to grab some fresh air.

# 10

"New video has arrived."

"How?"

"E-Mail."

"Any traces?"

"None. He knows computer very well. Just like the video editor thing, this email too comes from fake sources."

Raunak could feel the anger in Jasmit's words. The commissioner did not take a second to remind Raunak that the responsibility of the killings lay on him.

In the dark conference room, the video started playing in the presence of four to five people. Only the concerned team was allowed to view the video as everyone was skeptical that if the information leaked in media, media will take to thrashing the Delhi Police's image.

For the very first time, the video featured the face of killer. The moment everyone saw the face, they straightened their back in hope that something positive would come out regarding the investigation, but Raunak knew that nothing of that sort would happen. He was not negative about the case, but got to know the killer's psychology more than anyone else in the room.

"Year was 1988, somewhere in the mid of September, when he met the two most important people in his life. The year indeed was full of events for him and hence, he was ready for anything…." That childish face started narrating the story. Something was special about his face. He never looked horrifying. The one thing that Raunak noticed was the well-built structure of the killer. Childish face and heavy well-built body. Amazing combo.

Raunak was not paying attention today; he was lost somewhere. He always wanted to have a strong case, but now as he had it, he realized that he always ignored that there were lives involved in these cases. Some innocent people were getting killed for no sensible reason. For Raunak, this was the moment of truth. Then he heard something from the killer in the video, which grabbed his attention, instantly.

"For the first time, the child saw a naked man and woman, not just by clothes, but by their nature. Human behaviour was as pure as it should be. The city may have been sleeping, but this place was full of activity. The child was looking everywhere as if the Alice had come from her wonderland. But the most important part of all this was the lady that was holding the child's hand." Raunak heard this exact description of brothel for the second time in his life. If what he thought was

correct, the nightmare he had always lived would come to an end. But how can this be possible? Raunak, for the very first time, looked terribly afraid. He was sweating.

"A few policemen entered the room, and at the very moment, the man held the child's hand and pushed the lady out of the window from where she fell down on the ground floor and died." The video ended in an abrupt way.

"What the fuck these stories are all about? What the hell doe this person want from us?" Jasmit was angry and hence everyone else lowered their head. No one noticed the dumbstruck Raunak who was still looking at the screen, which had gone blank moments ago.

"Have we got anything on that truck driver's story yet?" Jasmit asked one of the inspectors.

"Sir, we are working on it. By evening we'll have the report."

"Report to me immediately, and grab some more men if you need." Jasmit stood up and then his eyes fell on Raunak.

"Raunak, are you alright?"

"He's my…." Suddenly, Raunak realized that this was not the moment to express his fear. "Just…. Just the tiredness."

Jasmit paid no attention to his words. He wanted to go berserk on Raunak, but then realized that he should not do this in front of everyone else. Raunak had a reputation and that should be maintained for the benefit of the department.

As soon as Jasmit left, Raunak ran to his apartment.

*"I want to talk about all this," his father said when the son decided to leave his room.*

*"But I don't," the son replied curtly. He usually was afraid of his father, but today, things were different.*

*"But how long will you stay silent? You should understand that it was necessary. We had no other choice."*

*"Don't use 'we' because I have my own choices and no one can stop me from having my choices." He said and left his room, leaving his father who was sinking his head in the table.*

*But his father wanted to confront this situation at any cost. He entered his son's room and saw him lying on the bed. He decided to sit next to him.*

*"Politics is a tricky business. You have to dedicate everything just to keep your name high. One dark spot and everything you did prior to it will vanish into thin air. People don't think about the positives you did for them, but will only talk about the negatives. That's politics for you in a nutshell and I hope you'll learn from what I am saying in coming future," his father said while playing with the hair of his son.*

*When he heard nothing from the son, he continued, "I had no other option left rather than taking him home. The world was cruel to him and maybe I was the last hope for him. I want you to understand that sometimes we are not the ones who make choices. God conspires to force us to make choices and maybe this choice I made,*

*was another of his conspiracy."*

Raunak sat in his cabin when this came to him as a flashback. Although he had no affection for his father, being a motherless child, whatever he had learnt in his life came from his father. Other children learn 'What to do' from their parents, Raunak learnt 'What not to do'.

That encounter between the father and son duo made Raunak decide that whatever happened, he would not join politics. He could never join such a thing that was based upon so many lies and deceit.

Lies and deceit, his father never told him from where and what was the reason that he was bound to pick that child up from the street who later became so called brother of Raunak, but he never knew that Raunak already knew the story from the child himself.

*"Don't try to spoil my life. I am his only love and if you tried to come in between me and my father, I'll kill you," Raunak said to the child when they both were alone in the room. At that very moment the father entered the room. First he kissed Raunak to sleep and then he went towards the child and pecked on both the cheeks. Raunak was burning. He just couldn't see the love getting divided.*

Each and every story related to his so called brother played in front of his eyes, but all in pieces. Raunak pulled the drawer of his table and picked the coin. Even the coin had its own story. He was looking at it keenly when the phone started ringing.

Before Raunak could say anything, the voice over the other end started, "So now I guess we are on the same page, brother."

"We can never be. You'll always be the other side of

the coin."

"Haha… are you talking about the same coin? Still having it?"

"Why you did this?"

"Because you wanted it. We both have suffered a lot; burnt in our own cells and this makes us equal now. You want answers to your questions. You'll have them," he said and hung up.

# 11

"Raunak.... Raunak?" His mind took around thirty seconds to recognize that the name belonged to himself. Slowly, he opened his eyes. His whole body ached. He tried to recognize the person calling out his name.

"What?" Raunak said, stretching himself up on the chair where he slept last night.

"We have got someone who knows our killer," Naveen said while standing in front of Raunak. Raunak's head ached still. Naveen's voice reached his eardrums, but the brain couldn't process its meaning.

"What do you want?" Raunak asked.

"Get your face washed with cold water first. I am waiting for you outside. Till then, we'll record his statement," Naveen said and left.

Raunak stood up, trembled a bit on the floor, losing balance, and then forwarded towards the washroom.

His head spun and it was unusual. This was not the first time he slept in his cabin, but he never felt this terrible in the morning.

He wished that the cold water would help, so without wasting a second, he leaned down below the running water so that it could fall over his head. It felt good. He stayed there for a few minutes and then helped himself to look presentable. Once done, he came out and stood next to Naveen as he took the statement of the person sitting on the bench.

"Sir, it was mere coincidence that I was also there in the parking lot when Rajgopal came down with the customer." The person was helping Naveen to record his statement and Raunak checked his details while standing at a small distance. "They were not looking as if meeting for the first time. No formal talk between them, nothing. The customer was moving ahead and Rajgopal behind him, and also Rajgopal was looking a bit scared. He was looking in every direction, maybe confirming that nobody is following. He even had a small knife in his pocket, I noticed he had one hand in his pocket. I was really afraid, Sir, as I had no idea of his intentions." Naveen had his ears on the person and eyes on Raunak. Naveen could sense that Raunak knew something about this man.

The man continued, "When they reached the car, the customer opened the back door of his car, pulled a bag out, and gave some cash to Rajgopal, which was way more than what the bill was. They exchanged some words, and then, Rajgopal came back and the customer left with his car."

Once done with the statement recording, when the man came out of the police station, Raunak helped him

by the collar from behind.

“Let's drink some tea.”

“What's your name?” Raunak asked while taking a sip of the tea. They both faced each other while sitting on the wooden plank that the tea staller offered.

“Ba.... Babban, Sir." The man shook in fear.

“Babban, have some tea. I am almost half done and you haven't yet started. It's good, try,” Raunak said.

Babban started to take long sips from the cup. “Babban, let me tell you a story.” Raunak felt as if he was experiencing Déjà vu. “There was a time when I needed a passport for myself and to prepare a passport, I needed a birth certificate. So, as I was born in a very small district of Haryana called Palwal, I reached the authorities there for my birth certificate. I was seventeen-years-old. Nobody listened to my pleas, just kept sending me from one table to another. Just like any other government work, they kept me on hold for more than a week's time.” Babban was confused as to why Raunak, a hotshot inspector, was sitting with him in the open, offered a tea and now telling this story of his birth certificate? But Babban kept mum as he had no other option. Raunak took a few sips and continued. “Then I met a Chacha. Someone introduced him to me as a distant relative. I liked that guy because he had solution for almost everything. I told him my problem and then he gave me a valuable lesson. He taught me to

recognize the 'Screwdriver' of the system. Do you know what screwdriver is?" Raunak paused to take one more sip.

"Yes, we use it to tighten the loose screw and...." Babban tried to reply to the most irrelevant question of the hour but was cut short in between.

"In every office, there's a person who is called 'Screwdriver' and the reason is he knows exactly when and how to tighten the loose ends. He knows everyone inside out. Regardless of his position in the organization, he can even bend the top officers according to his will. So, Chacha, on that day, helped me to recognize such souls." Babban felt uncomfortable, but Raunak carried on with his story. "So the next day, I went to the office, recognized the 'Screwdriver', offered him twenty Rupees, and within an hour, I was done with all the formalities."

Raunak took the last sip, snatched the half-filled cup from Babban's hand, kept it aside, and came close to Babban to ask, "Now tell me, why you were lying about Rajgopal?" Babban felt the floor disappear beneath his legs. Almost every part of his body started to shake in fear.

"Sir... Sir... no, Sir... Rajgopal... I... How can you say that I... I was lying?"

"Rugged jeans, yellowish T-Shirt whose original cover once had been white, oversized Jacket that must cost around 5000 to 6000. Having no purse, but keeping cash in such a large number that even your pocket is bursting out, and the most important thing is that cigar that you are using." Babban instantly puts his hand in the pocket of his shirt where the cigar was kept. "I can bet you don't have any idea about the cost of the Cigar

that your boss uses. You simply bartered it to tell a lie about Rajgopal." Raunak was filled with confidence. He loved to explain his hypothesis. "Now, will you start speaking or should I use other means? Because that Chacha has taught me many other lessons as well."

"Sir… Sir, I am a very small worker of the outlet. One day, Saab called me to his cabin and told me to recite this story in front of you people. Actually, Sir, he was bothered with the media reports. Everyone has started questioning the policy of protection of employees in an organization after Rajgopal's death. To maintain its reputation in the market intact, Saab wanted someone to turn the tables and portray Rajgopal as guilty."

"Tera saab toh gaya. Move inside and now record the correct statement We'll make sure that your Saab gets proper treatment inside the jail," Raunak said as he got off the wooden plank and pushed Babban towards the police station.

"Sir, please, sir please forgive me. These big people will not leave my family if they get to know about this. Sir please, I'll help you with anything, sir. Please, sir…." Raunak paid no attention to Babban and kept pushing him forward. "Sir, I can tell you one thing about Rajgopal sir. I have one information that could help you, sir, please listen to it." Raunak stopped. Babban continued, "Sir, the statement that I gave you people inside was not completely a false one. Rajgopal did know the customer that arrived at the store. They were friends, and because of some unknown reason, Rajgopal pretended as if he knew nothing about him when he arrived at the store. Sir, give me two days. I'll bring all the information about both of them. Just two

days. But please forgive me this time. I beg of you, Sir."

Raunak waited to make up his mind. He knew he was gambling and if this one betrayed him, he would lose everything that he had planned. But respecting his gut feeling, Raunak took Babban aside and told him everything.

"Listen, I am telling you something really important. If this information gets leaked, I'll not put you behind bars. I'll simply cut you in pieces." And then Raunak played the gamble and told him everything.

# 12

Jasmit Singh was facing a hard time. The media made his life miserable every step of his way. Calls from higher authorities across the nation mounted more pressure on him. He kept assuring everyone that the killer would soon be behind bars, but he knew he had no clue that could help him. The only ray of light was Raunak. It was irony for Jasmit. The one he hated the most would be the one to save his ass.

Naveen came rushing into the cabin without even knocking. Jasmit said nothing because he could sense the urgency in his footsteps.

"Sir we have got a breakthrough and you won't believe what we have found." Jasmit wasn't ready for one more shock, but the position on which he was sitting gives you no other choice.

"We tracked all the records, from across the nation, for the year 1988, and we got the reference to the truck accident here, in this newspaper cutting.

"Drunk driver faced the wrath of speed. Driver and the assistant died on spot." Jasmit read from the paper given by Naveen. He was confused. "But there's no mention of the kid here. How can we relate?"

"Sir, look at the date. 5th of September." Jasmit was not convinced. Naveen noticed on the expressions of Jasmit. He wished he could have been as convincing as Raunak. Deep under, Naveen did feel jealous of Raunak. Naveen tried one more time. "Sir, there is one more thing. Do you remember the next clip he sent? It was mentioning some police raid on a brothel. Here's the news."

Jasmit looked at another headline, stating some politician helping in the police raid on the city's biggest brothel.

"Now look at the date of this brothel case. 12th of September, 1988." Jasmit could see something revealing itself and what he was expecting was totally an eye-opener. "Even if we forget about the dates, just look at the place where the accident occurs and where this brothel was situated. Just twenty-three kms away. I don't believe in coincidences, sir. Do you?" Naveen said the last line and pointed towards the name of the politician written over the newspaper. Jasmit read it aloud, "Shankar Lal Upadhyay; father of Raunak Upadhyay."

"Why aren't you killing me?" the retired lawyer Karmaditya asked the person who imprisoned him for

so long.

"Because killing you will spoil all the fun and why the fuck do you want to get killed? I am not a murderer. I am just giving you the answers."

"What answers are you talking about?" Karmaditya was weak. He had no energy left, dying every day, pleading for forgiveness for something he doesn't know anything about.

"Tell me one thing." The man came near to Karmaditya and sat on the chair in front of him. Karmaditya was tied to the chair since the last seven to eight days. He actually had lost count of day and night. "Why do people help?"

"Out of humanity maybe? Out of…." Karmaditya tried to answer in a pretty low voice as he just can't manage to speak loudly.

"Humanity, that's the biggest lie we tell ourselves. There's no humanity out there. Being a lawyer, you should know that. I faced the true face of life at the age when most of the children learn to poop properly. Now tell me, why do people help?" He kept looking at his phone while talking with the lawyer. He seemed frustrated, for the very first time.

"Maybe in hope that the Almighty will see them doing the good deeds and help them when situations become vice versa."

"The karma concept," the man replied and laughed. "So you believe in Karma as well. Do you really believe in all the shit that you are saying? Who Almighty? Where was he when I faced this horrible life? Almighty, the fucking……" He was cut short by the lawyer for the very first time.

"I saved you from the death penalty. I saved you from many things that you could have faced. It is because of me you are roaming freely, or else for killing your father, you could have faced life imprisonment. I saved your ass by fighting for you because I knew what you have faced and under what circumstances you were forced to kill your father. I changed all your records so that you could lead a happy life after years of imprisonment, but you chose to live this life. It was all your decision." Karmaditya put all his energy in speaking it. He had surpassed the fear and just wanted to pour out the frustration he had. He did exactly the same. He felt lighter, but only for a moment.

"If you really wanted to help me, why didn't you save me on that day when you got to know the reality?" Karmaditya lowered his head, said nothing. He had no answers.

"By the way, I am thankful that you helped me and that's why you are here," the man replied, picked his phone and stood up to leave the basement.

"Please kill me."

"Eventually, you'll die. Believe me," the man said with a creepy smile.

"Shankar Lal Upadhyay, a big name in the politics. Almost anything happening in the capital had his name attached to it. He could have been the most powerful person on papers as well, but he chose the wrong leader

to follow. In his whole career, he stayed in the opposition party. It was….." The police inspector gave the brief on the projector with pictures of the politicians roaming around. Jasmit cut him short.

"Come to the point. I have no interest in his political background. Tell me about the family." Jasmit said.

"His wife, Sulekha Upadhyay, died in the very first year of the marriage. There were speculations that their relationship wasn't a happy one, but the way Shankar Lal named so many charitable events in her name, people were bound to believe otherwise. He had two sons, none of them biological. The first son was Raunak Upadhyay. Shankar adopted him from an orphanage after looking at the child's brightness. Raunak had an extraordinary IQ and…." Jasmit looked at the inspector with a straight face, which was the signal to skip and go forward. "The second child was Chandan Upadhyay. Shankar adopted Chandan from a brothel. If we try linking the story of Chandan with our killer's, Sudhir's story, we can conclude that Chandan and Sudhir, both are the same person, brother of Raunak Upadhyay."

"Where the fuck is this Raunak?" Jasmit shouted in between. Naveen came forward to answer, "We are trying to locate him, but his phone is switched off. Have informed everyone in the department, soon we'll have the information."

"Do you realize if he got hurt, media will kill us? If we can't save our own officers, how will the public trust us with their security?" Jasmit stopped yelling and signalled the officer to continue the presentation.

"Raunak was adopted when he was just eight and the very next year, Chandan got adopted. Things were

perfectly fine with everyone till 1996. One day, the security guard of the building in which they lived heard a loud thud. On inspection, he saw the dead body of Shankar Lal Upadhyay, who had fallen off the terrace. On the terrace, the security guard saw one child, Chandan Upadhyay. Chandan even confessed his crime."

"Wait a second. Chandan killed his father. Got arrested and came out of the prison as Sudhir Nagpal? How could that be possible?" Jasmit said.

"That's the point and that's where the last victim of Sudhir comes into the picture." He changed the slide and showed a lawyer in his attire. "This is Karmaditya, personal assistant cum lawyer of Shankar Lal Upadhyay. He had all the information about the system and was known as the right hand of the politician. Every advice, every decision taken by the politician, first got approved by him only. After the death of Shankar Lal, it was in the report that Karmaditya became the lawyer for Chandan. He spent hours before the police finally arrested him. And on the way to the jail, the police van faced a fatal accident in which all the inmates of the vehicle, burnt to death, including Chandan."

Jasmit understood but stayed silent to hear the story from officer's mouth. "If we track the records of Sudhir, everything mentioned over the file was false. Name, identity, people related to the case, each and every judge, everything was just a plan to save the boy from life imprisonment." Raunak had already told all this to Jasmit so he wasn't that surprised. The only thing that Jasmit was thinking was: why the killer killed all those people who helped him in his life? And where had Raunak disappeared off to? Was he the next victim?

And if not, was he also helping the killer in some way or another? Questions were many; answers seemed related but were far away from an explanation.

# 13

The next morning was unexpected for everyone. Jasmit stopped picking phone calls as he was panicking and had no answers. Naveen was shocked and was trying to coordinate with every unit possible. Chandan was still unaware that, for the first time, the plan that he had made so far was going to fall like dominos. Enthusiastically, when he opened a website to get the news of his plan getting fulfilled, he read something that made him shiver, as he was not ready for this.

Raunak's video as a new victim of the killer was getting viral over the internet. Without wasting a single second, Chandan opened the link and got redirected towards the YouTube link. Raunak was almost asleep in the video and someone was slapping him to keep him in senses. "Don't you want to hear a story?.... Hey, Officer! Raunak, let me begin, you have to hear this." Someone's voice was clearly audible but he didn't show his face. Video ended abruptly.

Chandan lost his control. Someone stole the show that he had set. Someone was destroying his plan. He just couldn't see Raunak lying there. Raunak was important as he was the main part of the whole plan. Chandan, for the very first time, shouted like a madman. His father was proved right once again. It's foolish to plan because if it fails, you have nothing left other than wait to face the consequences.

“This footage is morphed. Listen to it carefully.” The officer played the video of Raunak getting viral all over at ultraslow pace. “Did you head that?” Officer asked Naveen who was listening carefully.

“Yes, an overlap.” Naveen got excited. “Play it again.” Yes, there was an overlap on the video. “Can we enhance the background voice?” Naveen asked.

“One second.”

Now they can hear a complete change in the voice tone. “Pause it here. Rewind. Play.” The officer did the same. “I know this voice. I have heard this somewhere. But where?” He forced himself to remember, played the voice various times and then suddenly, a name popped up, “Babban?”

“Sir he worked at Big Bazaar outlet. He came here to report about what he saw at the parking lot. He was saying that he saw Rajgopal and Sudhir exchange some money, which was way more than the cost of his purchase,” Naveen said.

“There's some problem at this Big Bazaar outlet. Bring everyone, The manager, the owner everyone,” Jasmit ordered.

“But, Sir, the owner is the great industrialist...” Naveen wanted to say something.

“I don't care who he is. Don't listen to anyone, just follow my order. For the next seventy-two hours, this police department will work under no one's control. I want my officer safe and killer behind the bars in next seventy-two hours. From now on, we'll pick no phone call and whoever tries to stop, let me know. I'll file a case against them. Understood?”

“Yes, Sir!”

The police station was surrounded by media people, supporters of different political parties, college students, and some civilians. The situation had gone out of control for Jasmit. He had seventy-two hours only, or else, he had to resign as ordered by the CM.

The news of the arrest of industrialist Pawan Kumar spread within the city like forest-fire. The stock market fell, the city was almost on fire, but for Raunak, who was gulping down a chilled Coca-Cola in an

apartment on the thirty-sixth floor, listening to the news that Babban bought. All this was just news getting displayed over the news channel as breaking news. Fake and exaggerated. The real news was falling on his ears at that very moment.

"Even Rajgopal had a criminal record and guess where he was? In the same jail where Dharmendra Nath and Sudhir were kept. Coincidence? I don't think so, sir. Because Sudhir and Rajgopal both were the common customers at Ramu Desi Theka." Babban said. He laughed. "You won't believe but even Ramu was the inmate of that Jail only."

The moment he heard the name Ramu, Raunak couldn't stop himself from smiling.

Pawan Kumar was a big name and arresting such an influential person was not easy and hence the operation was carried forward in the wee hours of night. Jasmit knew that within minutes of arrest, phone calls from across the nation would start buzzing and hence he used the jammer in the vicinity. He wanted Pawan to start speaking within minutes and hence without wasting a single moment, the interrogation began.

"Who is Babban?" The name made his eyebrows flutter; he knew the name but acted cool.

"No idea."

"Then why did you plant him to provide us false information about the case of Rajgopal?" Jasmit asked

with a straight face and a firm voice. There were only a few people present in the room -- Naveen, Jasmit, the manager of the outlet, Pawan and his lawyer.

"You cannot put false allegation on my client." The lawyer came forward to make his point clear and Jasmit, at the very same moment, turned and slapped the manager hard. Everyone was shocked to see Jasmit's sudden reaction. The manager started to shiver in fear. He folded his hands in front of Jasmit.

"Start speaking now. Because I am in no mood of playing with you guys. My officer is in danger and the one who kidnapped him is Babban. We have solid evidence that you both know him. If you two think that we are fooling around, just think twice. Within hours media will start bouncing our name, politicians will start crying and everyone will have questions for us. If we did not have answers, we would not have taken such big steps. And Mr. Pawan Kumar, there's no chance of running away from here. For the next few hours, no one is coming for you, and if you think your lawyer can help you out so...." Jasmit turned towards Pawan's lawyer and slapped him hard as well.

"I'll.... I'll sue you, officer, I'll not leave you... you are using your powers wrongly...." The lawyer started to blabber but Jasmit paid no attention and simply looked directly into the eyes of Pawan. He was terrified.

"Now tell me, why did you send Babban here?" Jasmit was just inches away from Pawan. No one had ever slapped a lawyer. He could see the intensity of the scenario in eyes of Jasmit. Pawan had to say the truth or else, who knew, the next slap would land on his face as well.

"I… I did all this to save the image of the outlet. Newspapers and media were bouncing the topic among the commoners and the labor security rules and all this shit was killing business for us. This fucking manager, I had told him not to say a word in front of police, but they fucking don't have balls. Rajgopal died. I am sad for him. I compensated his family for it, but then, I am the one who is losing money on daily basis. There were talks everywhere that soon they will boycott every business of mine. Is that a joke? It took me years to create this empire. These fucking commoners think that they can destroy everything in a single day. Fuck these bastards." Pawan expressed everything but Jasmit still wasn't convinced.

"I am still looking for my answer. Who is this fucker Babban?"

"He is no one. Just an employee of my office."

"Then why did he kidnap my officer?"

"What rubbish? He can't do this. He's a fucking coward. I know him since last five years," Pawan said and Jasmit had to believe him because he couldn't see any agenda for Pawan to lie on this point.

"Recorded everything?" Jasmit asked Naveen.

"Yes, Sir," Naveen answered.

"Okay, so Mr. Lawyer. If you file a case against me or try to behave smart after leaving the premises, I'll leak this interrogation to the media. I don't fucking care what will happen to me, but believe me, this client of yours will surely see his 'Empire' falling." The lawyer kept his one hand on his cheek and nodded.

The manager, Pawan, and the lawyer left.

"What do you think, Sir?" Naveen asked the Commissioner.

"If I am not wrong, Raunak is in danger," Jasmit answered.

"Babban can harm him?"

"No. I'll kill this Raunak."

# 14

Chandan picked the phone. There was no signal. What could he? If he left this place, police could catch him, but he had to contact him. What if he got angry? He told me not to contact anyone. But without Raunak, what will he do? I needed to find him.

He picked the keys of his car and moved outside the jungle till he got the signal to make a call.

"Are you fucking crazy? Why the fuck are you calling?" the voice shouted just after picking the call.

"I want your help. You need to find Raunak."

"What? But police says that you have kidnapped him."

"He's not with me."

"What?"

"I want you to find him or else it will all go to waste. I don't know what to do. If Raunak is not there,

there's no use." Chandan's voice was shaking. The voice on the other side had never seen this face of Chandan. He felt the seriousness.

"You go back and let me find him. I'll call you when I get some clue."

It was not a regular day at the police station. Everyone was on their toes. Constable Vikram was ordered to bring some old files when he received the call.

"Hello."

"Vicky. Come out of the station right now and keep your mouth shut. Call me back on this number within five minutes." The line got cut. Vikram wasted no second in following the instructions because he knew exactly whose voice was on the other side. No one called him Vicky except Inspector Raunak.

He came out of the station. The darkness of midnight had surrounded the area but still, there was a lot of commotion of different media personnel. Somehow, he skipped each eyeball and reached the back of the station. He redialled the number.

"Sir, are you alright? Everyone's......" Vikram wasn't allowed to say anything, but was called to hear.

"Sunn, the parcel of videos that the serial killer used to send, you were always the first to see that right?" Raunak asked and Vikram suddenly felt the

fear.

“Yes, Sir, but I… I am not involved in this…. I…” Vikram was interrupted once again.

“I know you are not involved, but now you have to. Do you know Ramu?”

"Who, Sir?"

“Ramu Desi Theka, where you spend most of your nights. Listen now….”

“Sir, why are you doing this? Sir, I know I don't have a family behind me, but that doesn't mean I'll risk my life in this manner,” Babban said after listening to the instructions that Raunak gave to Vikram.

“Do you have anyone in the media who can help us in making news viral?” Raunak asked Babban without listening to what Babban was saying.

“I have, but what you want to make viral?”

“Your story. You, Mr. Babban.”

“Sir, why are you doing this, Sir? Why are you making me the lamb here? That is why I don't believe any policeman,” Babban stated.

“I promise, nothing will happen to you if you follow my instructions.”

“If I deny?” Babban asked and Raunak smiled. Babban got his answer loud and clear.

The place looked energetic. The clock showed one hour past midnight, but the level of enthusiasm of the place had no low. At the corner-most seat, Vikram and four new recruits were halfway down in consciousness. Vikram had a habit of drinking to that level from where he just couldn't walk back to his home on his own legs and that's why he always came to the shop with two or three companions.

"Since morning they are bothering us to do this and that.... Are we machines?" Vikram was shouting. He was not happy with his job just like the seventy-five percent of other police personnel. "Hey, waiter, bring one more Chivas...." The waiter rushed to Ramu, the owner, because he had instructions of letting the owner know if someone was drinking too much.

Ramu was ready to intervene when he heard a name, "Do you know who called me today? Raunak Sir called me today." Vikram said and Ramu stopped, instantly. "He could have called anybody, but who did he choose? Me. And this Jasmit thinks that I am good for nothing. Hey, waiter, are you bringing it or not?" Ramu picked a bottle and forwarded towards their table.

Vikram held Ramu's hands. Ramu felt a shiver pass through his body. "You tell me, Ramu. From how many years, do you know me?"

"Sir, around two years. You are one of our regular customers, Sir." Ramu smiled.

"Have you ever seen me this much happy?"

"Never," Ramu answered in one word as he wanted to just run away from the situation. He feared he would lose his cover.

"Today I am the happiest person in this world because only I know where Raunak sir is. And tomorrow, when I'll report it to the Commissioner, he'll promote me. I'll be an inspector then." He continued laughing like a madman. The moment Vikram left Ramu's hands, he instantly ran behind his bar counter. He made a satellite call and informed someone. The trap was set.

Vikram was going back home. His colleague left him on his society's front gate. No one noticed that the security guard was missing. No one noticed that the street light wasn't on. No one noticed that the street looked pretty quiet that night. No one noticed anything, but Vikram did. He was ready to take the danger as today he was not drunk. He was simply following Inspector Raunak's orders. He knew that from somewhere, someone will come and ask him the usual questions. The same thing happened.

Vikram just took a couple of steps towards his home after his colleagues left him when he felt the presence of four masked people running in his way. They all had knives in hands. Vikram got terrified.

"Where's Raunak? Tell us or prepare to die." One

of them threatened Vikram and Vikram started to speak like a parrot.

“37th floor, Kamla Apartments. Please leave me.” Vikram fell on the legs of the masked man. Vikram lowered his head and before he could pick his head up, all of them vanished into thin air.

“Sir, I have no idea how this information got leaked to the press.” Naveen bought his mobile phone on which the TOI app was open with news that shook Jasmit completely. It was the news of Raunak's kidnap. Finally, the fire had spilled out. The article was full of information about Babban. Within a few minutes, Babban became the new infamous celebrity of the town.

# 15

*He was mostly good to them and that's why they had no issue with what he did in nights. They accepted it as yet another lesson, yet another way of showing love. It did hurt. Yes, they cried but never wailed. The pain will make them stronger, he used to say. Although the piercing usually choked to death, somehow they survived for yet another night.*

Chandan knew he was dreaming, he knew he was sweating but couldn't move out of the bed. He could see his father's face in the mirror that was right in front of him. His father was standing behind him. He could feel that bone-shattering pain but said nothing. He wanted to be stronger, and for that, he had to face the burn, just like that coin. Now that the pain was getting unbearable, he had to do something. He needed to toss his body off the bed, somehow, and wake his body up. Chandan got restless. Though sleep paralysis was not new for him, every time he felt scared of it. It was not

something with which one could ever compromise.

Chandan pulled all the courage, gathered everything he had within himself, and then tried to jump his body up. In the first attempt, nothing moved. His father's eerie smile widened. Pain is the key, my son. He tried once again. Planning is the stupidest thing one can do. He pushed himself once again and this time, he succeeded in falling down the bed. His head hit the concrete floor and hence his vision got blurred out. Chandan had these illusions after such a long time and he blamed everything on his failure in planning.

When his vision cleared, he saw someone standing in front of him. Who could enter his place? Was it Karmaditya? But how could he escape the basement? Chandan's impulse reaction was to push away the person. But the person was quick in holding Chandan's hands.

“Are you alright?” It was Ramu.

“How did you come here?” Chandan asked while holding his head which was paining.

“Baba sent me here. We have to change the plan. You have to do it right now. Where's he?” Ramu was impatient, but not as much as Chandan was!

“But we need to find Raunak first. There's no point in doing anything without him. He is the main link in this whole thing.” Chandan explained his part. “How could Baba change everything at the last moment?”

“Things have changed. Our plan is no longer working. They already know what's going to follow. They have already 'house arrested' Raunak and also have caught that Babban. Everything that we did is now being celebrated by Babban. Haven't you seen the

news?"

A FEW MINUTES EARLIER

"Can't he just live without a cigarette? Damn!" Raunak was getting impatient and this was the first time ever in his life that he was losing his cool. Babban had no idea where Raunak had to lead his life. Although Raunak had clearly given instructions to Babban to not to leave the apartment, the need of a cigarette made him do what was prohibited. Now Raunak could only pray that he returned safely back to the apartment.

A sudden 'thug' made him jump out of the chair on which Raunak sat. He mentally counted the footsteps. It sounded organized. The only word that escaped his mouth was 'Shit!' before the gate flew open and dozens of men rushed inside to abduct him.

Raunak was feeling heavy on the head. He had no idea where he was. It was all dark, then he sensed that he was blindfolded. He shook his head in aggression, and when he did so, the blindfold was lifted. He could see many unknown faces in front of him, but only two were recognizable.

"Why did you do that? I was just close to finishing this case up." He embarked his opinion on Naveen and Jasmit.

"The case is already solved. We have arrested Babban." Jasmit said.

"But Babban is not the killer.... The real one is still on the loose and will strike again."

"We do know that Babban is not the real killer, but the city doesn't know that. You created Babban and we caught him. The city is happy, media is happy. And regarding the real killer...." Jasmit came closer to Raunak and continued, "Your brother, Chandan. We know that he needs you, and until the time you are here, he'll not do anything." Now Raunak understood everything. They had made the connection and now they would keep him house arrested until the time Chandan came out of the closet.

"How can you be so sure that he'll not do anything?" Raunak asked.

"I do believe that you have the answer of your own question and that's why you did all this. You knew that once the planning breaks, your brother feels paralyzed. It was all a calculated risk to bring out Babban from nowhere and project him as the killer. You knew that your brother cared about you and when you were in danger, he'd protect you and....." Jasmit was trying to clear out the clouds around, but when he heard Raunak's chuckle, he fell silent.

"He cares about me?" Raunak laughed harder. Naveen and Jasmit exchanged glances. "He hates me just like I hate him."

# 16

*The year was 1988 and I was happy with whatever I had in my life. I knew I was adopted and had to live with whatever my father would give me, but I was also determined to not follow in his footsteps. I didn't hate that man, I actually loved him. That day when 'he' joined in our family, I got to know that I was not ready to let my father leave my hand and hold another.*

*In the dark night when the lightning was on the verge of finishing this planet with a single blaze, he came in and stepped in my room with my father. I still can't forget those eyes; those wide eyes scanning me from top to bottom. He had some strange aura and that's what made me hate him from the very first meet. My father greeted him as my brother, but I considered him as my enemy with whom now I had to fight each and every day for the love of my father.*

*My father loved me the most and that I knew because he wanted me to be the strongest. Those night*

*lessons were important for every child. Though no child talked about it, but my father told me that every parent had a duty of making their children strong and that's why he always called me to his room at late nights. When the city sleeps, we had our session of drills.*

*The first time I felt awkward to get undressed in front of him, but he was as generous as to make me comfortable. He too stood naked. He then instructed me not to shout. That was the important point – not to shout. We could wail but in silence as he already told us that it would hurt. I had been made stronger mentally in the first few sessions and then one day he started. That pain was akin to bones getting crushed. But I wanted to be strong as the world outside would not treat me as an equal if I felt weak at this moment. I felt that my heartbeat was increasing and I was choking. I didn't shout. I remained silent, but then, I didn't know when I fell unconscious.*

*The next day he scolded me a lot, but it was necessary. These sessions were meant to make us strong. I was determined that the next day, I'd do better, and on that same day, 'he' came. I was afraid that he would replace me. I was afraid of him and hated him.*

*Thankfully, I didn't get replaced but got shared. One night, he trained me and next night he trained my so called brother. And that's how it carried on. I never talked with him. But whenever he tried, I either avoided him or hurt him badly by beating him mercilessly. He kind of enjoyed getting beaten up and that's why I feared him. He was stronger than I was. He got benefited of the training that my father gave but I was a slow learner. I blamed my father for that. I thought he loved him more than he loved me. He was getting some*

*special training.*

*One day I decided to sneak in the room when my brother was getting trained. It was dark inside but I could see them both. He was lying on bed with knee bended and two hands touching the surface and my father was standing behind him. I could see the face of my brother. He was smiling. Though he looked disoriented, with red face, hairs falling all over his face, covered in sweat or maybe tears but he had a smile on his face. That day, I saw his true power. I could never smile at that position. I knew exactly how painful it was but that child was smiling. There must be something that my father has told him but not me. For the first time, hate started to take over my mind for my father as well. I knew the world is merciless but I always thought that at least my father will stand with me but he was not. He was standing behind that son of a bitch.*

*Next day I decided to confront my father.*

*"Why is he so strong but I am not? Where am I failing?" I asked my father in front of everyone. He was in a conference room and we had clear instructions that the things that happened in the night will not be discussed in morning. But I did. I now had to be ready for the consequences.*

"We had our leads from the beginning, but were waiting for the perfect moment. Last night, we got the clue of his location and within minutes, our department reacted and now Babban is under arrest." The

spokesperson of Delhi Police was holding up a press conference to inform the city about the danger getting eradicated.

“What's the news about Inspector Raunak? We haven't seen him after the video. Is he alright?” one reporter asked.

“Yes, he is doing absolutely great, but after such trauma, we instructed him to stay at home for some days. He'll be back in the force soon," the spokesperson replied and the conference continued. Chandan decided to return the mobile to Ramu.

“Now you understand? Whatever we have done is now being laid to waste. We have to act now or else, it will go in vain.” Ramu was trying to convince Chandan. “Even Baba is worried that soon they'll find connection about everything and Baba will get convicted once again. He wants to see you succeed before everything gets to waste.”

Chandan kept quiet. Ramu thought that he got convinced and hence stayed quiet as well to give time to Chandan to think.

“Do you know why I am doing all this?” Chandan asked.

“Because you want to take revenge of whatever happened with you from childhood till now,” Ramu answered.

“Nope. I am doing all this because I want to tell Raunak that how important he is in my life,” Chandan replied and left Ramu wondering. “We believe in things what we can comprehend easily. You have seen the black and white, the good and evil, but I have seen greys all my life.” Chandan began to walk around Ramu. “I

have seen that in this world, there's no good. Everyone is pretending to be human, but actually, there's no one. The definition of human is wrong. We are just animals with a higher intellect. There's no difference between the wilds who are wandering outside and the one who is wandering inside in all of us." Ramu straightened his back, he sensed the danger.

"If we are allowed to do what we actually think, we'll do no good, we'll simply finish each other for what we love the most – that is ourselves. I have seen the world that is brutal and that's why I know humans much more than you do. Your Baba is no Guru, I know him what he actually is." Chandan was just behind Ramu and that's why Ramu silently slid his hand inside the shirt he was wearing to get the hold of the gun he was having.

"Baba knows how to use people like you, but he doesn't know how to deal with people like me and that's why he agreed when I told him my plan. Do you really think that I did all this because of him? Will I risk my life for that idiot who failed in his endeavour and now is thinking that he'll produce more like himself?" Ramu was about to pull out the gun and turn back when he felt a sharp pain on his shoulder. Blood oozed out from his hand and he couldn't stop streaming. Chandan had pierced his hand with an axe. "I did all this for Raunak." Ramu fell down and scrolled on the floor when in another blow, his hand detached from his torso.

# 17

*"Are you afraid?" That was the first sentence he said to me. His voice was pretty strange, much softer than what I assumed.*

*"None of your business." I reverted. We both were sitting under the blankets in our respective beds in our room. We had the most luxurious life any child can have. Our father was among the richest man of this country, someone once told me. Well, I didn't know what it means because I had never seen the poverty, for me it was all normal but not for him. I have seen the excitement in his eyes regarding everything he got after entering the house.*

*"What are you afraid of?" He asked again and I was getting irritated.*

*"Listen to me. It was all because of you that my life has become a living hell. It was not like this ever. You came and then this whole fucking problem of comparison came. I don't know why he discriminates*

*between us but I do know one thing that everything that will happen to me tonight is your fault." I snapped on him. I was pissed off as I knew that tonight would be different.*

*I heard footsteps approaching and with every step, my heartbeat increased. The gate opened and I saw him standing in front of us. He had that black belt in his hand and I knew what he'll do with it. Without any exchange of words, I removed my cloths and leaned back for him. He started beating me with the belt on my back.*

*"I know it hurts a lot but believe me son, this is important. If you want your future to be good, you have to learn how to behave in this society. I am your protector and it's my duty to protect you from the evil that is waiting for you outside the boundary of this mansion." He kept on swinging his belt mercilessly till the time few blood drops fell on the floor.*

*He then stopped, turned me to face him. He kneeled down in front of me. I was in tears. "Are you fine?"*

*I nodded. He continued, "I know what you are feeling and believe me it's absolutely fine. Brothers do feel jealous about each other but trust me; I never compared you with anyone. You both are my properties and it's my responsibility to teach you the lessons of my life." I looked at my brother. He was still in bed, poker face.*

*"Let me tell you one important lesson of life." He held my hand and took me in his room. I noticed that my brother also followed us.*

*He pulled a coin out of his pocket and showed me. "You see this coin; one side of this coin represents you*

*and another side of this same coin represents your brother. Both sides different, having different curves carved over them." We both were listening to him patiently. "These carves represents the struggles of your life till now. Both different, both unique."*

*Now he pulled a lighter from his pocket and ignited the flame. "This flame represents your father; that's me. My job is...." He started burning the coin from one side, "to mould you in such a way..." he then turned the coin and burned another side of it, "that both the sides, loses their own identity and become the same." He then showed me both the sides of the coin; identical.*

*"I am burning you at this moment of your life but I am doing all this for your own benefit. I am trying to bring both of you on the same page of life and stay strong so that no one can ever try to mess with you." He then kept the burning coin in my fist and forced me to hold the coin. "Believe in your father's plan and never question it."*

"Whatever the things are. I don't care about them till the city outside is safe and I am damn sure that till the time you stay hidden, your brother will not strike," Jasmit said in a firm voice and signalled all the men to leave the apartment. He too forwarded towards the gate.

"What do you mean by that?" Raunak asked in confusion.

"We'll keep you house arrested till the time we don't find your brother. We know he is having only a week's supply and after that he has to leave his hideout." Jasmit knew that Raunak would not like the idea, but he was the boss in this situation.

"You can't do that."

"Well, I did. Your apartment is surrounded by five of my men and they'll report to me whenever you'll leave. Believe me, Raunak, this is the best we can do at this moment. I am not doing all this on personal grudges, but this case is demanding much from us. I can't risk another life." Jasmit closed the gate on his back and left.

Raunak wasn't happy at all. He was furious and mentally weak to think a way out. He simply sat on a chair and pulled the coin out of his pocket. That coin was depressing for him, but at this moment, that was the only thing that seemed to be his companion.

# 18

*We ,the brothers, had one thing common. We loved the lessons of our father and the reason was the same, the fear of the outside world. I haven't witnessed but he did. I have heard stories of his survival and since then, my respect for my father increased in multiple folds.*

*That coin which wore the most important lesson of my life has now became the medallion for me. I started to keep it in my pocket every time. It reminds me of what I was preparing for. Days bygone and slowly my attention started drifting towards education rather than getting trained for the society. There's a strange thing about education and that is, it helps in opening the horizon of mind. Slowly the acts of my father started to seem wrong to me. My thoughts started to change and I started to refuse for the sessions of night.*

*For first few days, he simply understood me and replaced me with my brother. He still enjoyed the sessions, that smile was persistent. But after some more*

*time, my father started to lose control. One day, he came to our room fully drunk. His red eyes were indicating that something wrong was about to happen. He snatched the books from my hand and burned them. He then undressed me mercilessly and burned them too. I had no other option left but to stand there in silence. For the first time, he did his act in front of my brother. I was feeling the immense pain but my eyes were fixed on my brother. For the first time I didn't cry at all. We both kept on staring at each other's eyes. He said nothing. I said nothing; the only voice in the room was of my father's breaths and cursing. For the first time, all this look bad. For the first time I realized that what is actually happening with me. It was not any kind of training but was self-satisfaction. Father started screaming now, curse words were rapidly being thrown at us. I heard some disturbance outside the room but the gate stayed close. I could feel that other inmates of house, like maid, servant, and secretaries must have heard and maybe understood what was happening inside but no one interfered. I was expecting no one either. After around 15 minutes, I started feeling numb and maybe I passed out.*

He had no idea for how many hours he had stayed on the bed without doing anything, not even thinking. He had never felt such depression. He kept staring at that coin and trying to recognize where his side was. He kept on flipping the coin when he heard his phone ringing. Raunak wasn't sure whether he should pick the

call or simply keep flipping the coin but then, he decided to pick the phone.

"We are on the same page, brother. There's no side that belongs to me or to you." Chandan was calling from the other side and Raunak was wondering how he knew what Raunak was doing. He left the bed and searched the streets.

"I am nearby, but you'll not see me. The best option, if you actually want to meet me, is to follow the white van that is parked down the lane." Raunak said nothing. He noticed the van. "But be careful that nobody follows you."

The phone got disconnected and Raunak wondered where Chandan could be? He prepared to leave the apartment when he remembered the words of Jasmit. Five policemen were surrounding this apartment. He had to escape right under their noses. He continued looking at the streets for some time. There was no person wearing Khaki, which meant that they would be wearing civil clothes. Continued staring over the street made him aware of a few men who were trying to blend into the surroundings. He remembered their locations and after five minutes, he left the apartment. He used the less-travelled road to reach the van and escaped the eyes of those who kept watch over him. The moment he reached the proximity of the van, the van started.

Raunak started wondering how to follow the van when his eyes fell on the bike kept at the corner with keys on. Everything was set for him to follow the route and he did the same.

The driver of the van was pretty skilled; he was taking unnecessary turns just to make sure that nobody was following him on the trail except Raunak. After around half an hour, when he was satisfied that Raunak was all alone they rode towards the forest area in the outer skirts of the city. Raunak had no thoughts in his mind, just wanted to see where it would finally end. Suddenly the van stopped and the gate opened. Raunak thought that someone would get off from the van, but nobody came down. He then understood it was a signal to ditch the bike and get into the van.

Once he was inside the van, he saw a new pair of clothes and a blindfold. There was nobody inside the van to instruct him. Even the driver was absent. He did everything on his gut feeling. He changed all the clothes, threw out the old ones, and wore the blindfold. Once he settled, he heard three footsteps approaching. One occupied the driver seat and two surrounded him from behind. The van started. The clothes were special and within seconds, Raunak understood what exactly was happening and who he was going to meet now.

# 19

*It was all in flashes but I did remember that last time when I fell asleep, I was definitely not on bed. I was on floor, naked and exhausted. The pain was still green. I was finding difficulties in sitting and hence decided to keep on lying on my stomach. I looked at my brother who was sitting on a table, engrossed in some activity. Suddenly another flash of memory stroked me. I saw him naked as well, on the same night. Then slowly I remembered everything. When I passed out, someone threw water on my face after sometime. When I opened my eyes, I was in pain and hence decided to keep on lying in the same position; maybe I was bleeding as well. I saw my brother also lying at a short distance, naked which means that after I passed out, my father used him to satisfy his needs. But my father was nowhere, then who poured water on me and who made me sleep on the bed?*

*I decided to leave the bed as I was feeling thirsty.*

*Water jug was lying just next to where my brother was sitting. He was actually painting something using my colours. I wanted to snatch everything from him but was not in state of engaging in kind of fight. I just wanted water. I poured my class with water and when I was drinking; my eyes fell on the sketch he was making. In the middle, he drawn a coin and on the both sides of it, two boys maybe representing us. Now he was drawing something below the coin, maybe igniting on fire.*

*"Doesn't it look good?" He asked without lifting his head.*

*"That's pathetic." I replied. He smiled. "What is it all about?" I asked while sipping the last few drops.*

*"It's about our struggles, our fights which are helping us to be the same, to be the brothers, as father said." His voice was pretty strange and whenever he used to speak, he tends to draw attention.*

*"You believe in that shit?" I asked him in surprise. I wasn't expecting him to be that dumb but I couldn't blame him either, few days ago even I believed in that 'shit'.*

*"Do I have any other option?" He silenced me for a while. Then I asked him, "What's your opinion about father?" I don't know why I asked him but suddenly, it hit me to ask him. There are some moments in life when you simply don't want to do one thing but eventually you do the same. It was one such moment. I was discussing about a person who was once my life with a person who ruined everything in my life.*

*"I don't have any opinion. I am just learning and he teaches me well."*

*"Those sessions are not teaching, those are brutality. He is a monster." I said in low voice. I had fear that if someone overheard me, he may report it to father.*

*"Life is brutal. But you know what, it is better to see the brutality in home." He said and started drawing again.*

*I came back to my bed and tried to sleep again. It was difficult to understand a person who is so encrypted in himself. After sometime, he came and gifted me the drawing.*

*"I hope one day, we could understand each other and be on the same page." He said.*

*"That won't happen. Ever." I threw the drawing back on his face. He kept smiling. I simply hated him.*

"What's your thought about this, Raunak?" came a voice from somewhere. Raunak was finding it difficult to adjust his eyes according to the lights of the room. The blindfold had just been lifted. Slowly, his pupil dilated and he saw the old man standing next to canvas, drawing something on it.

Raunak knew that he'd land here and would see him. He walked in front of the canvas and looked at the painting. It was a child, surrounded by all the social evils of the world.

"I'll name it, the innocence, and guess to whom I'll

dedicate this painting?" Dharmendra Nath turned and faced Raunak. "Yes, you guessed it right; your own brother."

"So this is what you do now?" Raunak asked.

"Hm… well, I was a novice before. I always liked to draw but then your brother taught me how to, effectively, move the brush over the canvas," Dharmendra replied. He wore the white long kurta and pyjama with black strips running all over. It was a typical dress of every inmate of the jail. Even Raunak was wearing the same.

"You do know what I am asking about," Raunak clarified his question.

"I do know everything, Raunak, but please, let me take my time to reveal everything. I have waited for this moment for around fifteen years. Have patience." Dharmendra had a spark in his eyes. He was not looking the same as he used to look. He was more confident.

They were in a small room where there were no visible gates. Raunak had no idea from where he entered or where other people were. It seemed like a secret room in such a big premises. Dharmendra must have become a big name and have grabbed support from some big names around. The image that he creates outside, the 'being mental' image for just a cover-up. Raunak's eyes were continuously scanning the room in hope of finding something that looked odd. Dharmendra knew what Raunak was doing, but was confident about his planning.

"I always dreamt to become a name on which people can bank upon. A person on whom people could have blind trust. An image to look forward to. When I

was a child, I tried exploring my talents I wanted to know that what's in me that is unique and can help me achieve my dream. You know what I got? Nothing." Dharmendra Nath took a pause. He sat on the floor while Raunak was still scanning the room.

He continued, "People laughed at me when I sang, they laughed more I started dancing or started taking acting classes. I tried my luck in sports as well, but nothing helped. People kept on laughing; I lost my cool and one day… I killed a boy. I kept on stabbing him till his body stopped moving. No fear, no regret as I enjoyed killing him. The laughter stopped. Next day, the police came and took me as a prisoner. The day I got arrested, I had a smile on my face and the reason was the commotion I saw outside my house. The attention that the headline in the leading newspaper grabbed was the biggest achievement of my life. A 12-year-old boy stabbed his classmate to death. I became an overnight star." Dharmendra stopped talking. He was lost in the old memories. Now Raunak was slowly getting engrossed in Dharmendra's story.

"After three years, I escaped in the food truck from the prison. With a changed identity, I started living in Delhi. The best thing about Delhi was that everybody was so busy that no one asked me about myself. That thing helped me a lot, but also bothered me as well. I didn't want a life that went without ups and downs." Dharmendra kept on mumbling about his story when Raunak was mentally creating the escape route. He knew from which gate he entered the prison as when he entered, he smelt the garbage and also it was pretty obvious that they must have entered the premises from that gate where there was no CCTV; gate number 5, that was un-operational since 2012.

"I wanted to do something again and I knew where my expertise lay, but this time, I wanted to make it big." Dharmendra continued and Raunak continued making the map in his mind. 20 metres straight and then a right, two circles on spot then a left which meant heading towards the central library. "I wanted to get much more publicity than before. I wanted the world to speak and discuss me. That's why I used the medium which was the most popular one: the television. I decided to get in touch with media directly with the first clip of my masterpiece, but I knew it won't cool enough with just a murder. Have you seen a magic show, Raunak?" Raunak was busy in mentally calculating the path of escape.

"Raunak?" Dharmendra called his name again. "Don't overthink. There's no escape from here. Can't you see that there's no door anywhere? It's a trap from where no one can escape." Dharmendra chuckled on Raunak and then asked his question again, "Have you seen any magic show?"

"Come to the point," Raunak replied in frustration.

"I like that." Dharmendra laughed on it. He was enjoying the frustration of Raunak. "So in the magic show, the magician never reveals his trick in the first go. He waits. He tries to tell you about other things, he'll make you laugh, he'll create all the illusions, he'll try to distract you in every possible way till he has your utmost attention over what he wants you to focus. The same I did." Now Raunak was also paying attention to the voices around. There must be something that could reveal the place where he was. "I started telling random stories to my victims. I treated them as my audience and till the time they were agreed over what I wanted to tell

them, I never revealed my true intentions, and that's how I got the name of 'The Storyteller Murderer.'" Dharmendra was so proud of that name. The satisfaction about his past life was clearly visible on his face. "That name was the thing that I earned and I am so proud of what I did in my past life but then... you came to life." Suddenly the voice tone of Dharmendra Nath changed and he faced Raunak in a furious manner.

But Raunak paid no heed over his drama that he was creating. He just wanted to know why this place did not have any and was so brightly lit. It was affecting his eyes a lot. First, he thought that it was because of the blindfold but then he understood that it was actually odd. Mentally, he was still doing the left and right but nothing was making any sense. He was surely losing some data because according to his calculations, he should be in the activity area but this couldn't be possible because that area was the most crowded area of the prison.

"Let me tell you one thing, Raunak. You must be wondering, why I am telling this entire story. Well, if you have heard me correctly, the magician is doing his trick with you," Dharmendra said with an evil grin.

# 20

*The next few days were silent. Father doesn't come to our room. It was difficult to put him in any category. Sometimes he was bad, but sometimes, he looked good as well. He knew he committed mistake that day. He knew that he touched the extremities and that's why he was stealing eyes from us. For me the days were perfect but for my brother, he was not feeling good. He was feeling guilty about something or maybe he was missing father. He was lost in his own world. Always looking blank, outside the windows, wondering about nothing. But I said nothing to him. It was his fight, not mine. I was happy to see him lost. I was happy that I could focus on studies but life always takes U-turns. The same happened with me as well.*

*Commotion was high of people coming in and going out as well. Something important was happening in my father's life. We had the clear instruction of not watching or reading anything that relates to our father*

*but such things can't escape your ears.*

*"What did you say to him?" Father came in rushing our room and behind him there was a person whom we recognized as the personal lawyer of our father. I assumed that he'll come to me but he rushed towards my brother, which was actually a surprise for me. I must have trembled in fear after hearing the intensity of my father but my brother didn't even move. He had the stern eyes, looking directly in his eyes.*

*"Have I raped you? Don't you know what I did for you? From where I have bought you to my home? You fucking son of a bitch, I gave you the love for which you have craved your whole life and you tagged you as a fucking rapist?" My father started slapping him terribly. His side lip got cut and stream of blood escaped out of it. I had never seen him like that ever.*

*The person who was standing at the gates came rushing in to stop my father but my father even pushed him apart. "Sir, please stop. He said nothing. He did nothing. Please stop..." He tried a lot to stop my father but my father was in no mood to stop. I was pissing in my own pants.*

*"If he didn't say anything then how do you know about it? Did he complain?" My father pointed towards me and my worst nightmare came alive. He started rushing towards me and I tried to push the wall away so that I could escape out of the room but soon the man came in front of my father and hold him by hugging him.*

*"No he didn't. He was lying unconscious then. Why don't you understand? I was there when all it happened." Then I got to know that something happened that day when I passed out and the whole*

*problem that now we are facing is because of that day.*

*"What were you doing here and even if you were here, how dare you to question me and my life with my children?" My father now exploded the anger on him.*

*"Who am I? Don't you know who am I? Am I nobody for you?" The person got terribly hurt, emotionally. Both of us, the children in the room were silently watching this getting unfold.*

*"Are you getting distracted because of what we do in the room? Are you mistaking that act as the act of love?" My father said without even recognizing that he wasn't alone. We both were listening.*

*"We can talk about it later. Why are you..." the man started retreating while my father forwarded.*

*"Have you mistaken your identity? Do you think you have become the part of the family and are trying to save the children? Don't you know you all are just my puppets, more clearly, my sex puppets?" My father said and closed the gate. I was getting uncomfortable. The moment of truth was in front of my eyes. My hand instantly went inside my pocket where the coin was kept. I started flipping it inside the pocket and started thinking aloud that what exactly was happening here. The lies, the deceit, the cruel intensions, everything was in front of us. I was wondering whether my brother was having the same thoughts as well or not. His face was still bearing the poker look.*

*The man fell silent. I guess we all knew what to expect but I was not ready this time.*

*"Sir, the call came from the central prison. The call was encrypted so we had to use modern technology to crack the call." Naveen described to Jasmit while they were preparing to leave. They knew that Raunak was under threat and every angle was leading to the central jail and hence they decided to investigate by reaching there only.*

*"Did you track his movement?"*

*"Yes, we did, but we restrained ourselves from following him because the way Raunak was behaving, we knew that he was trying to escape our radar. After half of the journey, we lost the track of Raunak," Naveen replied.*

*"Why the central jail is in question? The jailor; Arman Malik, he was also the victim right?" Jasmit tried to recall.*

*"Yes, sir. He was the second victim."*

*"And Raunak was trying to build an analogy between Dharmendra Nath and our current killer, Chandan. He even said that he met Dharmendra in his cell and Chandan was in the same cell as well. I think that the case is trying to lead us towards the conversation they had: Dharmendra and Chandan. I just hope that we reach before anything happens to Raunak." Jasmit hurried with his squad.*

*In the whole mess-up, Chandan totally forgot about the living inmate of his hide-out. He rushed towards his basement in the hope that his inmate was still alive. Karmaditya lay unconscious over the chair. Chandan put his finger below the nose. He was alive, breathing but slowly.*

*Chandan threw some water over the face of Karmaditya and then offered him some water to drink. He was unable to move and hence he decided to help him out. Chandan wanted him to stay alive as he was the part of the game.*

*"How.... How long?" Karmaditya asked his question.*

*"Soon." Chandan replied.*

# 21

*You can change your life, anytime, anywhere but you need to take that decision; that one bold decision about which your mind was screaming tirelessly since the days started to worsen for you. Just a split of second is enough to change the course of your own and all the related people's life. That moment was priceless; the moment changed everything for me. I decided to run.*

*I was not ready to be the victim of it once again. I ran towards the closed door when my father was trying to get undressed in front of us. I knew I had to run away as fast as I could but I didn't notice that I also had to plan my way out. The main gate was obviously closed, so I had just two options. One was to roam around the house for no purpose at all and the second option was to run towards the stairs that would lead me towards terrace. I chose the second option.*

*The moment my father saw me running, he lost his control. He didn't expect me to do such thing and when I*

*did, he totally lost it. He picked his pants and without even properly wearing them, started running behind me. There were so many voices behind me that I stopped listening to any. But I do know that all three inmates of the room were behind me. I ran up without thinking anything, I just ran up. Opened the terrace gate and when I reached the corner, I stopped. Now what? This was the end. Sun has already lowered down and the light was just able to make its presence felt. I knew no one was coming to help me. The lawyer, was standing aside, doing nothing, from brother I had no expectations and my father was furious on me. I looked down. There were no chance of survival if I jumped, but there were no chance of survival either if I chose not to jump. What to choose? Where to go? Questions were many and I had to tally my options as fast as I could. My father was slowly moving forward. I stepped forward towards the edge and I heard 3 shouts, 2 were obvious but the third one wasn't. My brother shouted my name.*

*"Don't do that. There's no fun in leaving the battle like this. Have I taught you to run away like a coward?" My father started moving forward as slow as he could but eyes were not fixed on his movement but were on my brother.*

The moment Jasmit and his team reached the central jail, everyone came on their toes. Jasmit had every intention of meeting Dharmendra within the next few minutes and also wanted to meet every person

related to him.

Special arrangements were done as everybody knew that the matter was of high importance. The meeting was arranged for Jasmit and Dharmendra in a special cell.

"They said I had a visitor. I laughed on that." Dharmendra was quick to initiate the conversation. He was looking disoriented but still had a strange aura that attracted everyone around him.

"And why so?" Jasmit reverted.

"Because I know that my only admirer, Raunak, has been lost. and in no circumstances, he'd be coming here to meet me." Dharmendra's reply made things more complicated for Jasmit. Admirer? And how did he know that Raunak was lost?

"How do you know…." Jasmit was about to frame the sentence, but before he could complete Dharmendra cut him short.

"Raunak came here to thank me for giving him the case he deserved. But then I realized how small his wishes were back then. He actually had no idea how I felt that night when he came to me. I was a winner, but then Raunak came and took everything from me. I wished that I could finish him off using my bare hands, but thankfully I had a saviour next to me. His own brother. He is taking my revenge. You came here to find that fucking Raunak, you'll never find him. You have no idea what he is dealing with at this time. Even he has no idea. He'll suffer; he'll face the deadliest fate ever." Dharmendra started to lose his cool. A few men came rushing in and held him tightly. He was behaving like a wild animal. They escorted him towards his cell; the

darkest corner of the whole prison.

Jasmit got nothing from this conversation. He wasn't even allowed to ask anything. He came out of the room and soon Naveen caught up with him. “Sir, we have got the CCTV footage of the central courtyard, Raunak was there a few hours ago.”

Dharmendra was smiling as he looked at the clueless Raunak. Raunak was still unable to comprehend where he was. It was unlikely for him as he has trained himself in every condition possible, but this maze was invincible for him.

“Do you know why you are so important?” Dharmendra asked.

Raunak replied nothing, and hence Dharmendra continued, “Actually, you were chosen out of a lottery that your brother and I drew long ago. I was training him to continue my legacy, and also, I wanted to give you something more challenging to satisfy your ego. The choice was pretty simple for us.” Suddenly, Raunak's eye fell over a scar on Dharmendra's right hand. There was nothing unusual about it, but something clicked in his mind.

“Do you know what exactly I do in this prison? I brainwash the inmates and produce my army,” Raunak heard that and started laughing. “You can laugh, my friend, but do think that if I am cracking a joke then what the hell is your brother doing out there and why

was he behind you?" Raunak stopped laughing instantly.

"You think that prison helps us to improve, but no, my friend. There's no place in this whole universe where two evil minds can cancel the nature of each other. The criminals around us are like fuel, we just need to ignite them, and that's what I did with your brother. He told me his story and I gave him the perfect setting to create the havoc that could satisfy my ego. Your brother will work as a puppet and my name will come out in public, that was my dream but your brother spoiled everything for me. But don't worry, I am not like your brother. I keep my options open."

# 22

*This could have been the last moments of my life. I looked down once again to reconfirm that was I ready to do the blunder but then a voice from my head said that my life is already a blunder so I need not to confirm. I stepped forward and reached the ultimate edge of it. My father was trying to say something but I totally ignored him. The lawyer was afraid of everything happening around and my brother was doing something which was strange.*

*My brother put his right hand in his pocket, drawn something out and flipped in air. I tried to see attentively what he flipped but there was nothing. He did the act again and then I understood what he was suggesting but why? I was not ready for more questions and don't know, I did what he suggested me to do. I searched for the coin in my right pocket, took it out and flipped it in the air. My sudden change of behaviour surprised everyone. I started looking at the flipped*

*coin, my father tried to grab me and hopped towards me and within few seconds, don't know from where, my brother came running and pushed me aside. Sudden change in every position shocked us all but the most shocking thing was to see our father losing his balance and falling down the terrace. The darkest chapter of my life ended. But it ended with few questions. Why my brother did help me? He even confessed that he killed my father; even the lawyer was unable to save him. I saw him going to the jail. He still had that smile over his face. All I had was the coin which appeared the same from both the sides. Burnt coin that will keep on reminding me that the life I am living is a charity from the person whom I hated the most in life; my own brother, Chandan.*

"He was blindfolded when he was brought here, something happened in these few frames and then, Raunak lost his control over his body." Naveen was explaining the CCTV footage to Jasmit. "This all happened just 1.5 hours ago. If they are taking him somewhere out of the city, they must be within a 200 kms radius of this place."

"Seal the area and give clear instructions to everyone on the borders of the city," Jasmit ordered immediately. CCTV was still running and something grabbed the attention of Jasmit immediately. "Pause it; right here. What is he doing here?" Jasmit jumped off his chair.

"Dr. Virendra Tripathy? He is the psychologist who is handling the case of Dharmendra Nath and other such deadly criminals." Naveen explained.

"Arrest him now."

"The media attention, that's what I wanted from your brother but he turned all this as a personal vengeance. I am not here to assist him with the things that are personal to him but then he promised that he'll expose about the night when your father died." Dharmendra Nath said to Raunak. "Yes, I know about that night. Chandan told me about it and I also know why Chandan did all this. You still have questions, I have those answers. But as I told you earlier, I won't tell you everything that easily. I have a plan for you and you have to promise to be my puppet."

"I always knew that you were the smarter one because you always had plans but now when I am watching you getting crumbled down your own plan, I feel pity for you, son." Chandan could hear his father talking. He knew that he wasn't real, just a funny thing played by his own mind. Chandan was busy thinking what to do next when his father started talking.

"I know you never wanted to kill me and also you don't want to kill your brother as well. You just wanted to have a conversation with your brother and to have that, you created all this stuff but you never imagined that the game will go this way and all this mess around you.... How are you going to handle all this?" His father was authoritative, just like always.

"I'll do something; I have never failed in my whole life," Chandan replied.

"Yes and that's because your plans never failed you before but today, today the things are different."

"What do you know about me?" Chandan finally broke down. "You have no idea about my plans; I never planned when you were around. I thought that when you are there, I don't need to do anything. You'll take care of everything but then one day, I realized that everything around me was not normal and that one feeling made me do the unthinkable. I killed you."

"Do you regret?" Father asked.

"I don't know. I am not good with feelings."

"And that's because I never allowed you to feel any." His father replied. "For you the life was black and white, I gave you the grey but then you realized that too much of grey isn't that good for you and you revolted but even after your revolt, you were left with grey only."

Chandan stayed quiet as he couldn't comprehend his father's words.

"I taught you that we all are born different but our sufferings are the one that makes us equal in life. I was wrong. We are born different and are born so because of

a reason and that reason is just on the other side of the coin."

"But our coin was burnt, remember?"

"Even that coin is having the other side; you just have to rub it properly." His father replied and vanished into thin air. Chandan knew what to do next, the last act.

# 23

*"Don't let anyone know about you story, about your past. Believe me I can save you from all this. From now your new name is Sudhir Nagpal, I have written everything about your new life in this paper, simply read it and then flush it out in one of the toilet." Lawyer was whispering in Chandan's ear. They were in common room of the Juvenile prison. Chandan wasn't listening to the lawyer but was looking directly in his eyes. Chandan had few questions. From last 5 days that he had spent in solitude, he started asking himself questions and tried to solve the puzzle of his life. Why everything is happening? Whom to trust? Those eyes, full of question, that he saw of Raunak when he pushed his father from the terrace, forced him to think and now, Chandan only looks for questions, all around him.*

*"Are you listening? This all is important." Lawyer now looked at those eyes; those blank eyes of Chandan.*

*"Why you are trying to save me?"*

*"Because I can and I know what you have suffered." He was prepared with the answer. He expected such questions.*

*"Are you feeling pity over my life? Don't feel so. I know why all this happened; don't overthink. I can plan out my escape."*

*"But I can save you."*

*"If you really wanted to save me you would have saved me long before. You knew what we were suffering from. You are not trying to save me, but you are trying to save yourself. You are feeling bad because you did nothing on that terrace, you were sobbing like a kid and a kid like me solved the problem. It's all within you, that you want to save." Chandan leaned forward and that scared the lawyer. He never saw that kind of aggression in him.*

*Chandan continued, "In life I have seen one thing, there's no one out there who will come for your rescue and if someone comes forward, he dies. You are still alive and that means, you aren't saving me but you are saving yourself." Chandan's philosophy of taking shape and he believed in every bit he said, that was reflected in his eyes.*

*"Why are you doing this? Why you don't want to get saved?" Lawyer asked his last question before leaving.*

*Chandan said nothing. Just stared in lawyer's eyes for long, till the time he left.*

"So what will you do now? Seize my invention?" Dr. Virendra was sitting on the chair and was surrounded by the police officials. Everyone was shocked. "Oh! Wait. According to you, my invention is already seized, right?" Jasmit was looking right into Virendra's eyes. He had no clue what was happening in here. He thought that he had control over everything but the moment he has stepped in the central jail, everything seems to have fallen apart.

"Where is Raunak and how did you manage to even enter the premises without permission?" Jasmit asked.

"You won't be able to find the old Raunak now and the thing about permission; you think I need your permission to do anything? Just wait for few more minutes and you'll see the extent of damage that your silly decision has taken. What did I ask, huh? I wanted to save those people but your ego turned the tables for me and now I am helping these criminals in satisfying their ego and you know what? I love it."

"Whom are you helping? What have you done?" Jasmit came closer to Virendra.

"Dream simulator is here and the Raunak is experiencing the worst of it." Jasmit heard the words and started shouting like a maniac, "Search the whole area. Raunak is in here only. When you find him, don't try to wake him up and find him as soon as you can. Go… Go!" Everyone started running out but Jasmit stayed and held the collar of Virendra, "Why the fuck

you did all this?"

"I had no other option. When you said no to it, others said yes. My baby needed to see the world and for that, I could do anything. If not for the cops, it'll work for the criminals; but, it will work."

"Whatever my officer will face, I'll make sure that you face the double of it."

"How long have I been sleeping?" Raunak asked while rubbing his head. His head was spinning and it was difficult to focus on the person sitting in front of him. Although he knew that he was none other than Dharmendra himself.

"What do you think?" Dharmendra asked and then Raunak realized that there was no clock in the vicinity.

"It feels like months to me," Raunak said and while attempting to stand he felt the weakness. "Why I am feeling so weak?"

"As you said, you were sleeping here for months. All your energy has been drained out," Dharmendra replied and brought some water for Raunak.

"But this couldn't be possible." He drank the water in a hurry as he needed that badly. "You mean to say I have been here for months?"

"Yes. That's what your brain is saying."

"And you waited for me to wake up.... For months?"

"No. I just waited for few minutes."

Raunak was finding it difficult to comprehend. He was starving, lack of energy and tired brain; they were making him mad.

"Are you still looking for the exit?" Dharmendra asked.

"No. I am trying to figure out why are saying lies to me," Raunak answered.

"Lie? What kind of lie? Your brain can't lie to you."

"If I am in here for months then why that scar on your right hand is still green. I remember that scar, which I gave you when we first met. It's the same. Something is definitely wrong with this place and that's why I am unable to find the exit."

Dharmendra vanished into thin air for a second and Raunak saw some image; image of a dark place where he was bound in wires. He was lying on a bed and on his whole body, there were wires running all over. He even saw Dharmendra lying on the bed next to his. Soon the image vanished and Dharmendra came back in the room; the same white room and everything was normal again.

"Brilliant, Raunak. You are indeed a brilliant investigator. Now if I am not telling you about this place, that would be an insult to your intelligence and I'll never commit such kind of thing." Dharmendra started walking again. "The place that you are watching around you is made by me in the dream simulator. It's not real, but it's not fake, either." Dharmendra took a pause and turned to face Raunak.

"It's kind of a castle, which I made for me and it is

also a prison that I made for you, especially for you in my own mind." Raunak had an idea about the Dream Simulator, but he only knew the theory of it. He had no idea that such thing actually existed. "At present, your mind is attached to my dream and all the kind of emotions that you are experiencing are tailored by me. I have made this place, and using the technology, I am controlling your actions and emotions as well."

Raunak was shocked to hear it, but more shocking was the fact that he could do all this while staying in the prison? "In the shortest way, if I have to explain you would be that you are watching a dream that is tailored by me."

"But how..." Raunak wanted to ask but Dharmendra cut him short. "The right question would not be 'How' but 'Why'?" Dharmendra was feeling powerful; he had his prey in his jaws.

# 24

There was definitely someone out there in the bushes; a wild animal maybe who has smelt the flesh. Chandan was ready with his gun and slowly forwarded towards the main gate of the house. He had a blank mind and that's why he was attentive to each and every kind of sound. He could hear the breathing, someone was getting impatient.

The moment he reached the bushes, he knew what to expect and in a single move, he hit the head of the person trying to hide. Without any adieu, Chandan dragged the person inside and held the gun to his forehead.

"Who are you?" Chandan asked. The person was terrified to see a dead body lying. He knew the person; Ramu.

"I.... I was following Ramu, I am sorry.... Don't kill me. I won't tell anyone about anything."

"Who are you?"

"Please don't kill me. I don't know why I followed his orders."

"Who are you? And this is the last time I am asking."

"I am Vikram, a constable at Delhi Police. Please don't kill me. My senior, Raunak Sir, told me to follow this guy Ramu and I did so. I am…." Vikram was blabbering when Chandan cut him short.

"Where's Raunak? I want to meet him, can you help me out?" After hearing the name of Raunak, Chandan forgot everything. He actually had no idea what to do next. He tried contacting everyone, including Baba, but no one responded. He was clueless and then this Vikram came in.

"I don't know where he is but I do know who to ask."

Everyone was on the radar now. Soon all the government offices around Delhi had the news of what's happening in the central jail. But the secrecy of the matter was maintained because now, people actually wanted to sleep and such big news could have created havoc in the capital. Jasmit was given unlimited power to handle the case with care.

After half an hour's search operation, all eyes again turned towards the cell of Dharmendra Nath and when

the cell got opened, everyone was in shock as there was no one inside. A few torturous slaps on the face of Doctor Virendra were enough to know the exact position of Dharmendra and Raunak as well. Just below the cell, they had created a bunker for their research. It was clear that the bunker was made by only basic things because it wasn't well finished, but it also revealed that the many big guns were involved in all this.

As everyone descended in the bunker, they saw two beds lying next to each other and many wires running throughout their bodies attached to some central system which was unknown to everyone. On one bed, Dharmendra Nath was lying and on another one, Raunak. Jasmit felt happy to finally having Raunak in front of his eyes. He never felt this much happy to see the most annoying face of his life.

“Shut the machine down," Jasmit ordered Virendra.

“I can't,” Virendra replied and all eyes turned towards him. “If I forcefully shoot the machine down, they both will go into a coma. Dharmendra knew that you'll find them and that's why designed the dream in such a manner that if the machine got turned down in any manner, they both will go in a coma for an indefinite time.”

“So what's the escape?”

“There's none. Only Dharmendra can pull himself and Raunak off the machine.”

Jasmit fell silent as he was clueless what to do. Naveen was trying to understand everything, but nothing made any sort of sense, so he took Jasmit aside and asked, “Sir, why Dharmendra took Raunak in this

simulator? What is he trying to do? Eventually, he will get caught, what's the point of doing all this?"

"Dharmendra is playing his final act. Do you know what this simulator can do with your mind? It can redesign it and Dharmendra is doing the same. He is redesigning Raunak's thoughts and that's how he is going to take his revenge on Raunak." Jasmit looked tensed. He had to stop the machine, somehow.

"It all started when I was a child," Dharmendra stopped abruptly and looked at Raunak, "have you ever wondered, Raunak, that every story starts from the childhood only." He laughed at his own analogy. "So when I was a kid, I started enjoying killing. Well, wait, haven't I already told you this?" Dharmendra was getting confused. "Yes, actually I have told you all this; childhood memories. Even you must be having some, right? Memories that shaped you and your thoughts. Your brother had some. I loved to revisit all those memories with him in this place only. His childhood was indeed very depressing, even worse than yours."

Raunak was finding difficult to breathe. All his energy was draining rapidly. But thankfully, his mind was still working.

"I was really mad at you before coming here. I actually thought to give you the third degree, but then I changed my mind. Remember the year 2002? You were such a pain in the ass. After committing thirteen murders, finally, someone came who ignited fear

within me. I was afraid of continuing the streak, but then, I realized that it was difficult for me to give up on something which I loved the most. So I decided, if you are good at your work, I'll become the best. I planned my 14th murder accurately, but you were way ahead than me. For the first time, I felt defeated. All my hopes vanished into thin air and the time when I reached this prison…." Suddenly one thing struck Raunak. 'This prison, that means we are in the prison itself.' Dharmendra continued, "The only thing I wanted was to take revenge. For a couple of years, I stayed alone, thinking about every possibility of running away from this place and burning you alive. But nothing helped. I was disappointed but hope; I never left my hope."

Dharmendra took a pause, Raunak was still wondering how he got Dream Simulator and how can he escape the one. "But then one day, one God's own messenger came in my cell, Chandan, your own brother. The moment I realized that he is your brother; I got to know that even God wants me to take the revenge. It took me around 2 years to break the barrier he had created in his head. I made him realize that he could trust me. He did and then I started planning my quest."

"Baba, they called me as I used to teach them the philosophy of life and what their real person was in life. I used to speak shit and they believed because they had no other option. You know Raunak, when you are vulnerable, you trust anything. I created the devil in their mind and they, being vulnerable to society, became the threat to society." Suddenly Dharmendra stopped and turned towards Raunak and rushed to grab him.

"But why I am telling you all this? When I can show you everything." Raunak was confused. "Please permit me to show you the power of Dream Simulator." Dharmendra snapped his fingers and suddenly everything vanished. It was like the central stage getting replaced from one scene to another in a play. Now Raunak could see Dharmendra's cell in the prison. He was not looking at him but was looking at the other inmate of the cell. Both were facing each other but the other cellmate was looking down at the floor while Dharmendra was looking directly ahead on the wall. Raunak was finding it all difficult to understand but soon he realized that he was about see something and all he had to do was to wait.

"They all had to die, my friend. It was their destiny. They came in your life to teach you something important but unfortunately, you are still confused and may be reluctant to learn." Dharmendra said to the other inmate. He was sobbing while looking at the floor. He suddenly lifts his head to face Dharmendra. He was none other than Chandan himself.

"But why? Were they helping me right? Why did they have to die? That bangle maker, that truck driver, that lady I met on road, why? They just came in life and in the very next moment, they all died. The one person who didn't die, my father, I myself killed him? What kind of life is this?" Chandan barked upon Dharmendra and Dharmendra quietly listened to him, took a break and when he saw Chandan cooling down, he replied.

"They all came in your life to teach you something, a brutal lesson of life. You know Chandan, you are not an ordinary person. You are God's own child. You are sent to seek answers, not asking questions. Just think

what was common in all those people?"

"There was nothing common between them, except me," Chandan replied immediately.

"Yes, my friend. You were common among all of them. They tried to help you in one way or another. They tried to help a person who was God's own child. God wanted to let you know that he has sent you to earth to seek something and that 'something' will only be discoverable by you and for that, you have to travel alone. Whoever will try to help you, will get killed in the process because this is not about them, but it is about you, and just you."

Silence prevailed. After sometime Chandan asked, "But then why not my father?"

"You know that answer."

After some hesitation, Chandan said, "Because he was faking? He was not helping me but using me to fulfill his own lust."

Dharmendra smiled and then looked at Raunak. Again it all vanished into thin air and the bright, white room was back.

"So that was one of the many sessions in which I played with your little brother. He was easy to be moulded, but.... But one thing, which was difficult was, turning him against you."

# 25

With every ring, the heartbeat of Vikram was going low. Chandan was getting impatient, watching Vikram trying after every 30 seconds.

"Please pick it up, Sir. Please...." Vikram was chanting under his breath and Chandan was losing his patience.

"This would be your last try," Chandan announced and Vikram closed his eyes and dialled the number again. On the very first ring, Naveen picked the call and started abusing Vikram, "What the fuck is wrong with you?"

Chandan snatched the phone from Vikram's hand and started talking with Naveen.

"Nothing is wrong, at present, but if you don't connect me with Raunak in the next two minutes, your constable will die." Chandan took a pause and then continued, "And one more thing, I'll be live on your

favourite news channel in the next half an hour and announce the story of the fake arrest of Babban because the real killer is still out in the open and currently is talking over phone with Inspector Naveen."

Naveen was about to lose his grip over the phone but soon came back in sense. "You'll not do anything like that. You want to talk to Raunak, right? You'll have him…."

"In the next two minutes only or else your constable is gone."

"How… how can I arrange it in 2 minutes… please understand. Wait and listen…"

"1 minute 40 seconds." Vikram was about to start crying. Chandan was firm with his decision.

Naveen rushed to have a talk with Jasmit who was busy with technicians who were working to stop the machine on which Dream Simulator was working. Naveen explained everything to Jasmit and Jasmit, instantly grabbed the phone.

"Chandan, don't do this. We know everything about you and soon we'll even trace this call. You cannot run away now. It would be better to surrender and leave our man. This mistake would prove….." Jasmit was trying to play with Chandan's mind but Chandan was in no mood to give up.

"50 seconds."

Jasmit lost his composure and was trying to do something which could maintain the secrecy about Raunak but losing every argument.

"10 seconds. I think you don't want to see your man again."

"Wait, wait.... Raunak is here in front of us." Jasmit said and Chandan felt lighter. He lowered his gun and Vikram fell over the floor in relaxation. "But he can't call you because he is stuck in some machine. Dharmendra Nath, your cellmate has abducted him......" Jasmit was trying to make some sense in his words.

"Are you talking about the Dream Simulator?" Chandan asked.

"You won't believe me, Raunak, but your brother actually loved you," Dharmendra Nath started with his story again, "In this cruel world, you were the only person who actually hated him and that's what he loved about you the most. They say love is strange; it is actually strange and for Chandan, who had such a strange mindset, you were the complete puzzle."

Raunak lost his track of time and wasn't really appreciating what he was hearing about his brother. It was a kind of a shock for him. "For me, the most difficult thing was to turn him against you as his belief in you was really strong. Think logically, Raunak. His life was actually good with your father, but still, he killed him. Why?" Raunak had asked this question millions of times, but the answer was still nowhere. "He doesn't regret his life. After the death of your father, you both could have started a new life, but Chandan chose to stay behind the bars so that you can freely roam and live your life. Although it was all your fault, still

Chandan chose to sacrifice. Why?" Dharmendra was taking awkward pauses in his speech and those were his intentions. He wanted Raunak to think about the things that were unanswered and forgotten.

"How selfish you are, Raunak! Not even once you thought of all this?" Raunak kept quiet, but his head pounded. The questions kept hammering him. He tried to grab the coin kept in his right pocket but couldn't. The pain was now visible on his face. Dharmendra was enjoying the session. "Let me show you one more thing."

Surroundings changed again. The common area of the prison was now visible. At the far corner, below the shade of a tree, Raunak saw Dharmendra and Chadan talking. Raunak rushed near to them to hear the talks.

"I am amazed that even after so much of trouble; you still care for your brother."

Chandan chuckled at the thought and answered, "If we consider our age, I was the elder one, but because our father adopted him earlier, he used to claim himself as the elder one. Although he never considered me as a brother, I don't know why, I felt a connection with him. I don't care.... I am just thankful to him."

"Thankful? Why because he left you here to get rotten? Oh! My friend, grow up." Dharmendra was trying everything to change Chandan's view.

"It was not his mistake. I chose this life. Baba, the thing is, he was the only person who was true to me. He never came forward to help me nor did he stay back. He was the only person who came forward to hate me on his life. For the first time, I saw a strange kind of connection with him." He paused and then continued,

"I know I could have escaped the murder of my own father, but then what? What would I have done after that? I would have always stayed in fear of getting used again. So I chose to surrender. I would have done no good to anyone, so I chose to do good for my brother. I know he still has some questions for me and he'll never understand that we both were actually on the same side of the coin but let it be. The feeling that he had given me at those times, the connection that I felt with him that was more than enough for me."

"So you don't regret what happened that day on the terrace? The day when your father died?" Dharmendra asked.

"Regret? Why would I regret? I am thankful to my brother that he initiated the revolt that we deserved. He was the stronger one and he helped me escape that day. I hope that one day, I could confront him and say 'thank you'. I hope that one day; I could do anything for him. I just hope."

It faded again and the white, illuminated room was back. Raunak was now thinking nothing. He had no question left, just remorse for what he had felt for his brother all these years. The memories were back, the brutal days were back and all this was resulting in weakness. Raunak was feeling his soul getting shattered.

"Will you please shut this fuck up? What do you want from me?" Raunak finally lost his control. He wanted to escape now, anyhow.

"I thought it will take some time, but you, you are a brittle man. But sorry, Raunak, this is actually a suicide mission. So no turning back. That's how life works. You did your bit, I'll do mine."

# 26

“Believe me, only I can help Raunak.” Chandan was standing at the main gate of the prison; hands up and toes on the floor. Every gun in the vicinity had aimed the headshot of Chandan. 'This could be a trap' was the only thought in Jasmit's mind.

“Why should we believe you?”

“Do you have any other choice?” Chandan replied to Jasmit.

“But you wanted to kill Raunak, why would you save him?”

“I never wanted to kill him. I just wanted to face him and answer his questions.” Chandan wasn't afraid. He knew that nothing could go wrong from here.

“Fuck these brothers.” Jasmit cursed both of them under his breath.

Chandan continued, “Dr. Virendra, tell them I have

visited the machine earlier. You are not the person Dharmendra wants you to be. Don't follow him blindly, you never wanted to be the villain." Chandan looked directly into Virendra's eyes and was convincing enough to make him cry. Just because of lack of recognition, Virendra sold his invention to Dharmendra and now was regretting every bit of that contract.

"Commissioner sir, I am the only hope you have and, believe me, we don't have too much of time. Dharmendra is on a suicide mission. This was his plan B. I know every bit of his plan and I am the only one who can save Raunak's life."

Jasmit exchanged his glance with Naveen and then unwillingly ordered everyone to lower the weapon. I hope I don't regret in the same manner I did believe in Raunak's words. That's the only thought Jasmit had in his mind.

"This program is made in such a way that it plays with the victim's mind. It shows the memory of a person that he doesn't want to see and in such manner breaks the mental strength of the victim. There's a very simple way to come out of it, but when you are in, you lose common sense. The way to come out is to wake up," Chandan explained Jasmit and his team while preparing the machine.

"Raunak is inside the dream since the last five hours, which means, he has lost almost all of his mental strength which means waking up is not an option. So to

end the loop, I have to get inside."

"And how will that help?" Naveen asked.

"The thing is that this program is made inside Dharmendra's head, so whenever anything unplanned happens, the program will flicker for a second because the conscious mind will receive the signals and that's the time when you have to switch off the machine. Dharmendra would have planned everything, but not my entry into the program. So the moment I enter, you'll see their bodies shaking. The moment you see Dharmendra's or Raunak's body shaking, switch off the machine."

"Is that it?"

"Yes. That's it." Chandan was bit afraid, but didn't show to anyone. Dr. Virendra helped him with the wires and everything that was needed to enter the program. When everything was ready, Dr. Virendra put the mask on Chandan's face and signalled him thumbs up.

It took Chandan a few minutes to adjust and realize where he was. Like always, his head was spinning and the light was too bright all around. He was lying on the floor and hence tried to come on foot but finding it difficult. He was feeling drained out.

"Hello, my friend!" came the familiar voice. His fear was true. Dharmendra had planned his entry as well for the program, which meant no interruption, no chance of shutting down the machine. Chandan was

stuck as well.

"So you thought I would forget the love of yours for your brother? I thought that you knew me better." Dharmendra was sitting next to Chandan and Raunak was lying at the far corner of the same room. "So, Raunak, won't you like to see your brother, he's actually here. See, he's here to save you, again." Dharmendra picked Raunak up, who was lying almost dead, and threw him in front of Chandan.

Chandan saw Raunak after such a long time. Raunak was half-asleep; the dream simulator was sucking his energy.

"So, Raunak, I was telling you about Chandan only that how I made him stand against you. It was really a difficult task for me, but finally when you came up to see me in the central jail, you yourself helped me turn Chandan against you."

Things faded up again and with sleepy eyes, Raunak saw himself standing outside the cell of Dharmendra. He was watching another dream, but this time he knew what to expect as he himself was there.

"You don't have the slightest idea, Dharmendra, that how much I miss you. Since your case, none of the cases actually left me thinking. These criminals are so boring, their plan of action is so predictable, but you, you were the best. I hope that someday, someone will come who could challenge me with some good cat and rat chase. I came here to thank you. Thank you for giving me the case that I deserved." The young and stupid Raunak said and left. They say that be careful about what you wish for! The same happened with Raunak that day.

Inside the cell, Chandan heard Raunak and finally after so many years, he found something worth doing. He wanted to be the next Dharmendra for Raunak as he was ready for doing anything that could please Raunak.

It all faded again and the bright, white room was back. Raunak was finding difficult to breathe now.

"So that's how the story began. I actually wanted your brother to end up the things in the way we planned but plans don't actually work every time, so the smart person is the one who always keeps the plan B ready. So because your brother failed to complete plan A, let me end the story with plan B."

"Let me now take you to that same day, children," Dharmendra Nath faded and Raunak saw his father standing in place of him. The place faded and he was now in his room, in his childhood room. Raunak instantly looked to his right; Chandan was also there with no expressions at all. On the left, the lawyer stood with no shirt on. Everything was the same, even the fear.

Raunak could see the young Raunak running upstairs, everyone else also started to run. It was like a 3D movie running in front of him, but the fear was real, the fear of dying was real. Now they all were on the terrace. Everything occurred once again. Raunak pulled the coin out, swung in the air, father fell down, questions arose in mind and then it faded.

Raunak was now coughing. It was getting unbearable for him. Dharmendra came near to him, "How does it feel? How does it feel to die? I have felt this every day in that cell. Tell me, how does this feel?" Raunak was losing his consciousness when his eyes met Chandan's.

"Don't you dare to die, Raunak, you have to play with me. You can't just.... Die like this." Dharmendra was shaking Raunak's body vigorously when he started paying attention to what Chandan wanted to let Raunak know. Raunak focused on Chandan now. He was signalling him to put his hand in the pocket; the same pocket in which Raunak used to keep the coin.

"Don't die, please don't die, Raunak. I have waited for this moment since years...." Raunak stopped paying attention to Dharmendra's voice and started putting efforts to pull out the coin. With much energy, he finally reached the coin and flipped it in the air. The moment it happened, Dharmendra shouted.

"No......"

BLANK.

Jasmit and his team did fabulous work in identifying the exact point of turning the machine off. The flipping of coin was not programmed by Dharmendra.

# 27

It took Raunak ten days to recover from the effects of Dream Simulator and the first thing he did after the discharge was paying a visit to Chandan.

The person with whom he shared nothing the entirety of his life and hated the most had now saved his life. How would he counter him? How would he ask him about the questions that were so obvious? Raunak was finding it difficult to even face Chandan.

"Do you know I hated you the most in my whole life?" Raunak chuckled upon the situation without looking at Chandan who was sitting just opposite to the table that was lying between the two brothers.

"And do you know that's what I liked about you. No one hated me just the way you did," Chandan replied and that made Raunak look at that innocent face. They said nothing but the eyes did all the talking.

"Only if you had tried to convey your feelings to

me, this would not have ended up like this." Raunak broke the silence again.

"Things would have been different, but the person can't. Destiny is pre-written, brother. Nothing can be changed, nothing can be altered. Our life is not in our hands, it's actually in our mind and who knows who controls this mind?" Chandan was trying to smile at his own philosophy and Raunak joined him. For the first time, they both were smiling. Life is actually unpredictable.

"I have some questions," Raunak asked.

"I know. You can ask them all."

"What was your deal with Dharmendra Nath?"

"Hm… I knew his plans from the very beginning. Life has taught me that when some stranger starts to take lots of interest in your personal life, start doubting and I did the same. I got to know his evil intentions of killing you and I also knew that he is having some great connections so the only way out that I could see was to play the card of the victim. I told him my story from beginning to end and made him believe that I will work for him. You may not know, but inside the prison, he had his own little army. Dharmendra was not a good leader. He could influence you, but can't lead you to do something for him. So I played along."

Raunak was listening to all this very patiently. "I made him believe that I would follow his trend of killing people and make him popular once again. He was mad about popularity. So to make him believe, I picked my first target Rajgopal Datta. He was the constant supplier of Dharmendra. He was actually our supermarket. Whatever we wanted at the prison, he

used to bring that up for us. I killed him in the same manner as Dharmendra used to do but I kept a distance from media because my target was to meet you, not to follow any legacy. I guess that's where Dharmendra started to doubt my intentions and started working on the Dream Simulator."

"My second victim was our Jailor. He knew everything that was happening inside the prison but kept mum because he had enough money in his mouth. I decided to permanently shut him up." Chandan took a pause and before he could start, Raunak asked.

"But then why Karmaditya? He was innocent, right?"

"I didn't kill him. He is safe. I just wanted to answer his question. He had asked me, why are you doing this? Why don't you want to get saved? So I showed him my circumstances; the situation where death seems lovely but you have to live. I didn't want to leave any question unanswered. He was a spineless man, why would I kill him?"

Silence prevailed.

"Don't you want to ask about the day when I pushed the father down the terrace?" Chandan asked.

"No. Now I do understand you. I think we are now on the same side of the coin." Raunak replied. Chandan looked up at his brother and couldn't stop his tears falling down.

# EPILOGUE

Dharmendra Nath and Dr. Virendra both received their own Karma from the Indian Penal Court. Babban got released and the first thing he did was barking on Raunak and crying in front of him. Raunak decided to hire him as a personal investigator for future cases. Chandan was happy to have his brother who visited on every Sunday. He was finally getting what he deserved, happiness.

Raunak got suspended for a month. Jasmit got promoted and Naveen was still getting help from Raunak in different cases.

Whenever Raunak gets free time, he does think about his father and what could have been done on that day when he ran on the terrace? Could there be any other way of running away the situation that got created on that day? Even now when these questions arose in his mind, the decision was left on the same coin that resides in his right pocket. He still flips it in the air and tries to figure out the other side of the coin.

The end